DARK DESIRES

A NOVEL

THE SWISS OBSESSION

NAREN LOKWANI

Om Books International

First published in 2025 by

Om Books International

Corporate & Editorial Office
A-12, Sector 64, Noida 201 301
Uttar Pradesh, India
Phone: +91 120 477 4100
Email: editorial@ombooks.com
Website: www.ombooksinternational.com

Sales Office
107, Ansari Road, Darya Ganj,
New Delhi 110 002, India
Phone: +91 11 4000 9000
Email: sales@ombooks.com
Website: www.ombooks.com

ISBN: 978-93-6395-506-6

Printed in India

10 9 8 7 6 5 4 3 2 1

DARK DESIRES

Naren Lokwani holds an MBA from the Indian Institute of Management (IIM) Bangalore and an Electronics Engineering degree from the National Institute of Technology (NIT) Jaipur. With over 20 years of extensive work experience across the US, Europe, India, and the Middle East, Naren has established himself as a versatile and seasoned expert in the software industry. He is also an accomplished author, having published a management book on rapid software development, available on Amazon. Currently, Narendar channels his vast knowledge and expertise into his role as a software entrepreneur, driving innovation and excellence in the technology world.

Naren Lokwani is the author of the insightful book *Startup Idea to MVP in 12 Weeks*, a practical guide designed to help entrepreneurs transform their innovative ideas into market-ready products swiftly. This book, available on Amazon, combines his extensive experience in the software industry with actionable strategies, providing readers with a step-by-step roadmap to navigate the complex journey from concept to Minimum Viable Product (MVP). His work is a valuable resource for aspiring startup founders, offering clear guidance and expert advice to accelerate their path to success.

For your feedback on this novel, please drop a note to narend@gmail.com.

Dedicated to Sadhguru, whose wisdom inspires us to embrace creativity, embrace life, and grow into better versions of ourselves every day.

Contents

CHAPTER 1

The Shimmer of Her World

Anna stood in her art gallery in Zurich, a home for creativity and luxury. Dressed in a button-down shirt and tailored trousers, her hair neatly pulled back in a ponytail, Anna looked like the picture of an art professional.

"Mrs Harrington! How lovely to see you," Anna said, lightly shaking the hand of the lady dressed in faux leather, her shoulders pushed back and her head scanning the walls for art pieces.

She guided Mrs. Harrington to a newly arrived avant-garde painting, with its bold strokes and daring colours. "This piece," Anna began, "is by a rising star in the art world. It's not just a painting; it's a conversation starter, a statement of boldness and vision. Imagine it in your collection—a symbol of your impeccable taste and style."

Mrs. Harrington's eyes flickered with interest. Anna continued, subtly weaving the artist's compelling backstory with the painting's unique attributes. "The energy, the passion—it's almost palpable, isn't it? This isn't just art; it's an investment in the future of creativity."

As Mrs. Harrington's gaze softened and her lips curved into an appreciative smile, Anna knew she had succeeded. The allure of the painting, coupled with Anna's enchanting narrative, sealed the deal. Within minutes, the painting was sold, and Anna basked in the glow of another successful sale for her gallery.

Anna was born in a small Swiss village, Grindelwald, nestled in the Alps. With her reddish-brown hair that went down her back in waves and her striking green eyes that sparkled with intelligence and curiosity, she was a picture of natural beauty.

Her charm was effortless, and her posture was very confident. Anna's childhood was a blend of growing up in Swiss country landscapes and a good upbringing from her parents. Her father was a local artist, well known for his intricate wood carvings, while her mother ran a moderately successful bed-and-breakfast hotel that attracted tourists from all over the world.

Anna spent her early days exploring the beautiful forests and mountains of the Swiss countryside and interacting with the guests who stayed at their inn.

From an early age, Anna showed a keen interest in art. She would spend hours sketching the stunning scenery around her, and her drawings used to capture the elegance of Swiss country life.

Her parents supported her talent by enrolling her in art classes and encouraging her to pursue her passion. By the time she was a teenager, Anna's artworks were already being displayed in local galleries.

It was during her time at the University of Zurich, where she studied Art History, that Anna met Hans. Hans was an established author, and was invited to speak about the intersection of literature and art at Anna's college. Anna was swayed by his presence, and loved his deep voice that was resonating with confidence and authority.

Hans, by this time, was already a successful author. He was equally taken by the beautiful young Anna, who asked insightful questions and showed a genuine love for art.

Their relationship blossomed quickly. Hans was enchanted by Anna's beauty and Anna was equally drawn to Hans' intellect. They complemented each other perfectly, their love story unfolding like a fairy tale.

Soon, they married in a cosy ceremony in Anna's hometown, surrounded by family, friends, and the breathtaking beauty of the Swiss Alps. Their love story had a great start.

Their early years together were filled with happiness and adventure. Hans' career was at its peak, and Anna's career in the art world was beginning to take off. She became a respected art dealer and started a thriving Art Gallery, fuelled by her talent for business and her ability to discover new art talent.

As Hans' books climbed the bestseller lists, Anna's art gallery also thrived. They became the golden couple of Zurich social circles, and were rich, smart and sophisticated. They purchased a beautiful home in Zurich's posh area, Fluntern, which was the home to the old-moneyed Zurich residents.

Their home soon became a melting point of intellectual and artistic activity, filled with writers, artists, and critics. Anna and Hans travelled extensively, attending book launches, art exhibitions, and literary festivals across Europe.

In short, they were the envy of everyone's eyes and were on the lips of everyone in Zurich's high society!

As the years passed, the initial excitement in their marriage began to fade. Hans became increasingly busy with his writing, often working in his study room for days on end. Anna, on the other hand, found herself growing bored and lacking stimulation in her life. The vibrant social life they had once shared was replaced by long periods of boredom and silence.

Anna sought excitement in her work. She threw herself into her role as an art dealer, curating exhibitions and forging connections with artists and collectors. Her art gallery soon became the most successful and popular place in Zurich. It was the place where art's who and who were displayed, and top art transactions took place.

It was also a place where Anna could escape the monotony of her personal life.

Her days were filled with meetings, phone calls, and endless emails. She spent her evenings at gallery openings, mingling with Zurich's elite. She built a network of influential friends, people who shared her passion for art and her appreciation for the finer things in life. Her parties were extravagant, the conversations stimulating, and the champagne flowed freely.

Despite the success and the glamour, Anna felt a growing emptiness inside her. The spark that she once shared with Hans had dimmed, now replaced by a life of loneliness and longing. She missed the late-night drives, the shared excitement over discovering a new restaurant, the never-ending shopping and travel together, and the exciting sex life of their initial days with Hans.

Hans had ceased to become the exciting and stimulating person he appeared to be, when she had first met him in her college. His increasing work-load only deepened the divide and heartburn between the once lovely couple.

He was consumed by his struggles and impending failures, and was completely ignorant of Anna's pain. She would come home late, often after a night of socialising, only to find him tired and asleep in his study, surrounded by empty whiskey glasses and scattered papers.

Their conversations in the mornings were superficial, and their interactions lacked any warmth.

Anna began to seek solace elsewhere. She found herself drawn to the nightlife, the glitz, and glamour of Zurich's social scene. The parties provided a temporary escape, a way to fill the void that had grown in her heart.

She danced under the shimmering lights, laughed at jokes of the men around her, and engaged in a flirtatious manner with them, all the while trying to hide the sadness in her life. She also formed close bonds with a few select friends, people who understood the challenge of her life and offered her sympathy and time, something that Hans lacked.

There were nights when Anna would return home late, the city's lights still twinkling in her eyes, and she would find herself standing in front of Hans' study door. She would listen to the sound of his typing, the rustle of the papers, and the clinking of his whiskey glass.

She would reach for the door handle, wanting to step inside, to speak with him, but the fear of rejection always held her back. The distance between the two of them was slowly becoming insurmountable.

Anna's life had now completely become a whirlwind of glamorous art openings and exclusive social gatherings. Her art gallery she had poured her heart and soul into was a thriving business now, and her reputation as an experienced and honest art dealer was well established in Zurich.

She loved the vibrant energy of the art world, finding solace in its beauty and chaos, which provided a relief from the dull life she lived at her home.

As she navigated the social events, Anna couldn't help but notice the attention she garnered from younger men. The young men of Zurich party circles admired Anna for her sophistication, business success, and social grace. She felt a sense of excitement and vitality in the company of these men that she had not experienced in years at her home with Hans.

The idea of social flirting was both thrilling and exciting, and was a tantalising escape from her monotonous life. She felt the excitement of engaging in flirtatious chats with the exciting party boys of Zurich nightlife, which provided her the rush of feeling desired as a woman again.

These fantasies danced on the edge of her mind, flirting with the boundaries of her reality, as she wondered how far she might allow herself to go.

Anna enjoyed the subtle yet intoxicating touches she encountered at the art galleries and evening parties. The light touch of a young man's hand as he handed her a glass of champagne, the gentle pressure of a cheek kiss, or the lingering warmth of a handshake. All these gestures sent shivers of excitement through her body.

She found herself enjoying these encounters, replaying them in her mind, and delighting herself with the thrill of being desired and admired by the young men.

Anna found herself increasingly amused by the devotion of her intern, Arjun, who was studying European art history at Zurich University. His hungry stares and eager-to-please attitude were a constant source of entertainment for her. She mischievously enjoyed the way his eyes followed her every move, with his admiration for Anna plain as day.

Anna often caught herself wondering just how far Arjun would be willing to go if she gave him even the slightest encouragement. Would he become her lapdog, ready to obey her every whim, blinded by his infatuation for her?

The idea entertained her, adding another layer of excitement to her otherwise predictable life. She found Arjun hanging on to her every word, doing anything to earn her favour, and the thought brought a sexy smile to her lips.

One evening, at an especially glamorous gallery opening, Anna found herself in a conversation with a strikingly handsome young Swiss artist named Lukas.

He was everything Hans had forgotten to be–vibrant, enthusiastic, and utterly captivated by her. His eyes sparkled with admiration as he hung on her every word, and his laughter was infectious.

They spent the evening talking about art, life, and dreams. Lukas had a way of making her feel seen and appreciated, a feeling that had long been absent in her marriage. As the night went on, the conversation took on a more intimate tone. They moved closer, the distance between them shrinking with every word, every shared smile.

At one point, they found themselves standing in a secluded corner of the gallery, away from the prying eyes of the crowd. The soft glow of the lights reflected in Lukas's eyes as he looked at her with an intensity that made her heart race.

He reached out, gently brushing a strand of hair from her face, his delicate touch sending a shiver down her spine.

"Anna," he murmured, his voice low and inviting. "You are enchanting."

Her breath froze as he leaned in to kiss her, his lips dangerously close to hers. For a moment, time seemed to stand still. The noise of the party faded into the background, leaving only the two of them, suspended in a moment of possibility.

She felt an overwhelming urge to close the distance between their lips, to lose herself in the warmth and excitement of Lukas' wet lips. But at the last moment, she pulled back. Lukas looked at her, a flicker of disappointment in his eyes, but he quickly masked it with a charming smile.

"I understand, Anna," he said softly. "But if you ever change your mind, you know where to find me."

Anna nodded, her heart pounding. The encounter left her shaken, a stark reminder of the sexual void in her marriage and the easy allure of the extra-marital affairs.

As she drove home that night, the city lights blurring past her, Anna couldn't shake the memory of Lukas's touch and the way he had looked at her. The temptation was strong, and she knew it would only grow stronger if the gap between her and Hans continued to widen.

Anna reached home and quietly made her way to her bedroom, slipping under the silk covers and staring up at the ceiling. As she closed her eyes, she let her hands wander down her own body and instead imagined Lukas's strong, gentle hands exploring her body. She cupped and massaged her ripe bosom, played with her now taut nipples and imagined Lukas' lips sucking her breasts.

Every thought of his whispers and the way he made her feel desired sent waves of pleasure through her. She sighed deeply, losing herself in the fantasy, her mind and body responding to the vivid images of Lukas and the longing he ignited within her.

With a soft moan, Anna began to take her hands down her body, pleasuring herself with her two wet fingers. The sensations between her legs grew more urgent as she imagined Lukas's touch. She imagined Lukas was going down on her, and she was holding his hair and forcing him to lick her deeper.

She hadn't had sex for many weeks, and the pent-up desire heightened her imagination and sensitivity. The maddeningly slow pleasuring of herself built an intense pressure inside her, causing an explosion of pleasure in her head.

The blood rushed to her cheeks, painting them with a flush of crimson colour. Her breaths quickened, and her body tensed as the waves of pleasure grew stronger.

The climax hit her like a tidal wave, her entire body shaking as the pleasurable orgasm washed over her, leaving her breathless and spent, with a serene smile on her lips. She found herself uttering the name of Lukas over and over again, as the massive orgasm shook her body.

As she lay there spent, she resolved to push Hans to try to rekindle the flame that had once burned so brightly between them. But deep down, she feared that it might already be too late, and the fractures in their marriage were beyond repair.

CHAPTER 2

Shadows of a Fallen Star

Hans Keller sat in his study, surrounded by the memories of what was once a successful career as a novelist. Manuscripts, half-written and discarded, were lying scattered across the floor of his study room. The cursor on his laptop screen blinked mockingly on a blank document, a silent proof of his creative paralysis. Outside, the glamourous skyline of Zurich city seemed to add insult to his injury.

The study room was a mess, much like his life. Bookshelves, once organised by genre and author, now held a chaotic jumble of titles. His desk, now cluttered with coffee-stained papers and empty whiskey glasses, stood as a proof of his growing despair.

Dust gathered in the corners, lying undisturbed for months. The study room, which had once been his peaceful sanctuary, now felt like an unkempt prison cell for Hans.

Hans' days had fallen into a monotonous routine. Every morning, he would enter the kitchen, make a pot of strong coffee, and sit at the kitchen table, staring blankly at the newspaper. The headlines from the paper blurred together, no news sparking his interest or imagination.

He would somehow manage to eat a bowl of cereal, its lack of taste matching the dullness in his chest. After breakfast, he would force himself to go to his study, hoping that today would be different.

But the words never came. He would sit for hours, fingers poised over the keyboard, only to give up in frustration. His study, once a place of boundless creativity for him, was the place from which he had delivered many successful and superhit novels.

But now his study buzzed with an unbearable silence. The blinking cursor was his enemy, a constant reminder of his inability to produce any meaningful manuscript.

All through the day, Hans would wander through his beautiful and empty Zurich house. Often, his footsteps were the only noise in the house. He often would find himself in the living room, staring out of its large bay window.

The view from his house was breathtaking and glamourous. The serene waters of Lake Zurich shimmering in the sunlight were easily visible from his house. The distant Alps were standing majestically against the horizon, and he would often sip his coffee looking at the beautiful Swiss mountains.

But even this beauty couldn't penetrate the fog of his despair. He would spend hours watching the world go by and not making any progress at all. Hans had tried everything to break out of his writer's block. He had read countless books on getting out of writer's block, attended workshops, and even meditated, but nothing worked for him.

The thrill of creating intricate plots and complex characters, which he was a master at, had now vanished, leaving behind a void he couldn't fill. His mind was a barren wasteland, devoid of ideas and stories.

His marriage was another impending disaster in his life.

He and Anna had grown apart over the years, their once passionate relationship reduced to polite conversations and awkward silences. She was always busy with her art gallery, attending exhibitions, and mingling with clients, while he was left alone with his thoughts.

The distance between them was growing by the day. Their conversations were now routine chats about grocery lists and household chores. Any real connection with his life partner had evaporated quite a while back.

Hans simply did not know how to get his life back in order.

Before this writer's block hit him, Hans had been at the top of the world. His novels were international bestsellers, translated into multiple languages, and adapted into blockbuster films.

His books like *The Swiss Files, Zurich Shadows*, and *The Alpine Mission* had dominated international bestseller lists. Agents and movie directors used to chase Hans relentlessly, eager to secure the rights to his next novel. He made a lot of money for all of them, when his books were selling well.

Hans remembered his glamorous book launches, the exhilarating book tours across Europe, and the intoxicating thrill of seeing his stories come to life on the big screen as movie adaptations.

He had once enjoyed the love of fans and even the praise of his critics. His past life was a whirlwind of literary success and celebrity status. The memory of standing ovations at literary festivals, the flashing cameras, and the endless autograph requests now seemed like a thing of a past life.

He recalled the thrill of his first book launch at the prestigious Zurich Literary Festival. The room had been packed with eager readers, critics, and journalists. Hans had read an excerpt from *The Swiss Files*, his voice charming and confident.

The long applause that followed had been thunderous, a sound he could still hear in his mind. That night, he partied hard with Anna and felt invincible. He was certain that his success would never go away.

But now, that seemed like a distant dream. The calls from agents had long stopped, the invitations to literary events had dried up, and the movie directors had forgotten him. Hans was no longer the celebrated author; he was a man lost in the shadow of his past glories. His email inbox, once flooded with requests for interviews and discussions, now contained only spam emails and pending bills. His finances were in tatters. Hans took another sip of his coffee.

One night, driven to the edge by another rejection letter and a particularly vicious argument with Anna, Hans thought of ending it all. The thought of suicide, which he thought of as the option reserved for the cowards, seemed like the only way out for Hans.

He found himself standing on the edge of the top balcony of their house. The cold wind buzzed around him as he looked down. The city of Zurich glittered like a jewel. The distance between him and the ground seemed to be the right distance for a quick end to his torturous life.

He closed his eyes, imagining the jump, the silence of a few seconds while he went down, followed by a quick contact with the concrete road below. A few seconds of pain will relieve him of years of boredom, neglect, humiliation, and failure.

He felt a strange sense of calm, a clarity that had eluded him for months. He took a step closer to the edge, the cold metal of the railing supporting his movement forward.

But as he stood there, on the edge of nothingness, a small voice inside called him out. The voice reminded him of the love he once felt for Anna, the joy of their early years together, and the pride he took in his novels. It was a whisper of hope, a reminder that even in the darkest times, there was something worth holding on to.

Tears streamed down his face as he stepped back from the edge, the realisation of what he had almost done. He lowered himself back to the balcony and stayed there for what felt like hours.

In that moment of profound vulnerability, Hans made a silent vow to himself. He would not give in to the darkness, no matter how tempting it might be.

He would find a way to reclaim his life, to rebuild what had been lost. It would be a long and difficult journey, but he owed it to himself, to Anna, and to the memory of the successful novelist he once was. Hans knew that the road ahead would be fraught with challenges, but for the first time in a long while, he felt a glimmer of hope.

He would face his demons, confront the conflicts in his marriage, and find a way to rediscover his passion for writing. It was a faint light in the darkness, but it was enough to guide him forward. With a deep breath, Hans walked back inside, closing the door on the cold, dark wind behind him.

CHAPTER 3

The Domestic Battleground

The early morning sunlight filtered through the transparent curtains and cast a warm glow over the Keller household.

Hans sat at the kitchen table, his face covered with weariness as he nursed a cup of black coffee. The newspaper lay open in front of him, but the words blurred together as his mind was unable to focus on the news.

Anna went around the kitchen, preparing her breakfast of fresh fruits, wheat bread, and Swiss cheese. The scent of freshly brewed coffee mingled with the aroma of toasted bread, a nostalgic reminder of her simpler times.

"Did you remember to pick up the dry cleaning?" Anna asked to have a conversation with unusually quiet Hans.

Hans looked up, his eyes dull. "No, I forgot. I was working late last night."

Anna sighed, her frustration evident. "Hans, I asked you to do one thing. I have an important meeting today, and I need my suit."

He rubbed his temples, feeling the familiar tension build. "I'm sorry, Anna. I'll get it now."

"It's too late," she replied, her voice laced with irritation. "I'll just have to manage with something else."

Anna continued her breakfast preparation, and the chopping of the knife was the only sound in the room. Hans stared at the newspaper, and his mind was deeply involved with his thoughts.

Later that evening, Hans sat in his study, attempting to work on his latest novel. The words came out slowly, and forming each sentence was a struggle for Hans. This was a far cry from the eloquent and talented Hans, who had given so many successful novels in the past.

He could hear Anna in the living room, talking animatedly on the phone with one of her clients. Her laughter rang out, a stark contrast to the silence that enveloped him.

He sighed and leaned back in his chair, staring at the ceiling. The once familiar comfort of his study had turned into a prison, and the white walls felt that they were closing in on him. He longed for the days when writing had been his refuge, his escape from reality. Now, it felt like a burden and a constant reminder of his failures.

The sound of footsteps approaching broke his thoughts. Anna appeared in the doorway, and her expression was tense.

"Do you have a moment?" she asked, her tone tense.

Hans nodded, gesturing for her to come in.

She stepped into the room, her eyes scanning the cluttered desk, the empty whiskey glass, and the mess of paper sheets lying all over the room.

"We need to talk," she said, with her voice firm.

He braced himself for the conversation he knew was coming. "About what?"

"About us," she replied, her gaze unwavering. "We can't keep going on like this, Hans. Our marriage has to improve."

Hans felt a surge of defensiveness. "What do you mean? I'm doing my best."

Anna's eyes softened slightly, but her resolve remained. "I know you are, but it's not enough. We're drifting apart, and it's affecting everything. Our home, our work, our relationship."

He looked away, unable to meet her gaze. "I don't know what to do, Anna. I feel like I'm losing everything."

She took a step closer, her voice gentle. "We need to find a way to reconnect, to remember why we fell in love in the first place. We can't let this distance grow any wider."

Hans nodded slowly, the weight of her words sinking in. He wanted to bridge the gap, to find a way back to the love they had once shared. But he didn't know where to start.

As the days turned into weeks, the tension between them only grew. They argued regularly over household chores, finances, and their respective careers.

Hans felt increasingly isolated, and his frustration was manifesting in bursts of anger. Anna, in turn, became more withdrawn, seeking solace in her successful art gallery and her busy social life.

One evening, after a particularly heated argument about their now deteriorating finances, Hans stormed out of the house, as he wanted to clear his head.

He wandered through the streets of Zurich, the cool night air doing little to calm his nerves. The city, with its blend of old-world charm and modernity, seemed to laugh at his inner turmoil.

He walked past the elegantly designed shops, but their grandeur was lost on him. Turning left, Hans found himself on Rennweg, a narrow, charming street with roads made up of artistic cobblestones. The buildings here were historic, with their beautiful details and colourful shutters offering a glimpse into Zurich's rich past. He continued walking aimlessly, passing cosy Swiss cafés and small, inviting shops, their signboards swaying gently in the evening breeze.

As he reached Lindenhof, an ancient Roman fort turned into a peaceful park, Hans paused for a moment. The view of the Limmat River from the elevated park was breathtaking, the water reflecting the city's lights like a mirror.

He took a deep breath, trying to absorb the tranquillity of the scene, but his inner storm persisted.

Continuing his journey, Hans made his way down Niederdorf, a lively street in the old town known for its vibrant nightlife and eclectic mix of bars and restaurants. The sound of laughter and clinking wine glasses reached his ears, which was a stark reminder of the joy and companionship that seemed so distant in his own life.

As he wandered through Zurich's streets, Hans couldn't shake the feeling of being lost, not just in the city, but in his own life. The cobblestone streets, historic landmarks, and vibrant nightlife offered little distraction from the storm within.

His walk through Zurich, a city of beauty and tradition, mirrored the tumultuous path his life had taken, leaving him to ponder the next steps in his increasingly dark journey.

After wandering for what felt like an eternity, he found himself standing on the banks of Lake Zurich, the water shimmering under the moonlight. He stared at the reflection, feeling the weight of his failures pressing down on him. The distance between him and Anna felt insurmountable, a chasm that grew wider with each passing day.

Meanwhile, Anna sat alone in the living room, tears streaming down her face. She replayed their argument in her mind, the hurtful words echoing in her ears. She wanted to believe that they could find a way back to each other, but the reality seemed increasingly bleak.

Their domestic life had become a battleground, each day a struggle to maintain a semblance of normalcy. They fought over the smallest of things – the dishes left in the sink, the forgotten grocery items, the misplaced keys.

The intimacy that had once defined their relationship was now a distant memory, replaced by a cold detachment.

One night, after a particularly lavish gallery opening, Anna returned home to find Hans sitting in the living room, a glass of whiskey in hand. His eyes were red-rimmed, a testament to the sleepless nights and the strain of their constant arguments.

"Where have you been?" he demanded, his voice slurred with alcohol.

"I told you, I had a gallery opening," Anna replied, her tone weary.

Hans slammed his glass down on the table, the sound shattering the silence. "You're always out! You don't care about our marriage anymore!"

Anna's frustration boiled over. "And what about you, Hans? You're always locked away in that study, drowning in your misery!"

The argument escalated quickly, their voices rising as they hurled accusations at each other. The tension that had been building for months finally erupted.

In a fit of rage, Hans grabbed Anna's arm, his grip tight and unforgiving.

"Let me go, Hans!" she cried, struggling to free herself.

He released her abruptly, his face contorted with anger and regret. Anna stepped back, her eyes wide with shock and hurt.

"Is this what we've come to?" she asked, her voice trembling. "This is not the life I wanted."

Hans turned away, ashamed of his anger. The room fell into a tense silence, the weight of their conflict hanging heavy in the air.

The tension in the Keller household slowly reached a boiling point. Their arguments were a nightly occurrence and resembled a toxic everyday ritual that left both Hans and Anna emotionally broken. Yet, beneath the anger and resentment, there lingered a primal and physical attraction, twisted and distorted by their mutual hatred for each other.

It was on one particularly stormy night that this toxic mix erupted into a physical encounter neither of them would forget. After a particularly vicious argument about finances and Anna's late nights out, the air was thick with unresolved anger.

Hans stood in the living room, his fists clenched, his face flushed with rage and hatred. Anna glared at him from across the room, her eyes blazing with fury and hurt. Without warning, Hans crossed the room and grabbed Anna by the shoulders, his grip tight and unyielding.

"Is this what you want?" he spat, his voice low and dangerous. "To push me until I break?"

Anna's heart raced, her breath coming in short, sharp gasps.

"What I want," she hissed back, "is for you to stop wallowing in your self-pity and fight for something. Fight for us!"

The words hung in the air for a long time, and it was a challenge that neither one was willing to back down from. In a moment of impulsive passion, Hans pulled her closer, their lips crashed together in a brutal and hungry kiss.

It was not the tender, loving embrace of a married couple, but a clash of animal wills, with each person trying to dominate the other. They stumbled to the bedroom, shedding their clothes with a mix of desperation and anger. The sexual act that followed was a twist on their former intimacy.

Hans's act was rough, and his sexual movements were driven by a need to reclaim some semblance of control. Anna responded similarly, with her actions fueled by a desire to hurt him as deeply as she felt he had hurt her.

The sex was angry, hurtful, and aggressive, each thrust towards each other a manifestation of their pain and frustration.

There was no tenderness, no love, only a desperate need to relieve themselves. The room filled with the angry sounds of their bodies colliding, their gasps and moans mingling with the loud wind outside.

Their torn clothes lay in a heap on the floor, a proof of the intensity of their physical encounter. Fabrics were ripped and buttons were scattered all over the place, and clothes were mingling together in a random pile.

When the sex was over, they both lay side by side. Their bodies were covered with sweat, and their breaths were coming in gasps. The bitterness in the air was apparent and was a stark contrast to the physical closeness they had just shared.

Hans turned away, staring at the ceiling, his mind awash with conflicting emotions. He felt no satisfaction, only a hollow emptiness that seemed to echo the void in their relationship.

After this bitter encounter, Anna retreated to the bathroom, seeking solace in the warm embrace of a bath. As she lowered herself into the steaming water, the sharp sting of physical pain made her wince.

She looked down and saw the bruises blooming on her skin, harsh reminders of the roughness of their desperate encounter. Her body ached in places she hadn't noticed in the heat of the moment, and the sight of the bruises on her skin made her stomach churn with a mix of anger and sorrow.

The physical pain was a stark contrast to the tender caresses she had once known from Hans, which were now replaced by the violence of their broken love.

As she gently washed her body, her tears mingled with the soapy bathwater. Each drop of water was a testament to the deep wounds, both physical and emotional, that had been inflicted on each other.

She felt used, betrayed by her own desires, and felt the harsh reality of their situation. The memory of her time with

Lukas flashed in her mind, a reminder of what true intimacy felt like.

Hans lay in bed, the aftermath of their encounter leaving him in a state of disarray. As he stared at the ceiling, a twisted part of him found a perverse satisfaction in the physical hurt he knew he had inflicted on Anna, mingled with the self-loathing he felt for his brutality.

The rawness of their exchange had stirred something deep within him, a dark thrill at the power and pain they had shared. Yet, this fleeting sense of control was quickly overshadowed by guilt and confusion.

The enjoyment of their mutual suffering left a bitter taste in his mouth, further blurring the lines between love and resentment, pleasure and pain. As he lay there, Hans couldn't shake the unsettling desire to repeat this sex experience. The shame of his actions was apparent, but beneath it lurked a simmering anger.

He was furious that Anna seemed to find solace and happiness in her work and social life while he drowned in his failures. His career was in shambles, his creative spark extinguished, and each day felt like a reminder of his failure.

The thought of Anna finding joy, of her moving on while he remained stuck, festered within him, fueling his resentment further. He wanted to hurt her again, to make her feel the same despair and helplessness that consumed him. The physical act of their encounter had given him a sense of power, a fleeting moment where he wasn't the only failure.

It was a dark, vicious cycle, but the anger and bitterness clouded his judgment. In his twisted state of mind, the idea of causing her pain became an outlet for his frustrations, a way to assert some control over the chaos of his life.

Hans knew these thoughts were wrong, that they only served to deepen the divide between them. But in his desperation and rage, the lines between right and wrong, love and hate, became increasingly blurred.

The darkness that had taken root in his heart threatened to consume him, driving him further away from the man he once was and closer to a path of self-destruction. But it wasn't just physical domination that enticed him. Hans wanted to break her spirit, to see the light of happiness fade from her eyes.

He fantasised about psychological games and subtle manipulations that would leave her questioning her sanity. He thought about planting doubts in her mind, making her believe she was the one responsible for their fractured relationship.

The idea of watching her break, of seeing her confidence and independence crumble, was intoxicating.

Hans's mind wandered to the darker corners. He considered involving other people in his twisted fantasies, using their presence to humiliate Anna further. He imagined inviting someone over and then forcing Anna to endure his sexual cruelty in front of an audience to ensure her humiliation was complete.

Each dark thought was a way for Hans to assert control in a life that felt increasingly out of his grasp. The fantasies provided an outlet for his rage and frustration, a way to channel his feelings of inadequacy and failure.

Yet, even as he engaged himself in these twisted plans, a part of him recoiled in horror at what he had become. The man who once took pride in his creativity and compassion was now consumed by a desire for power and vengeance, and his love for Anna twisted into something unrecognisable.

Despite the shame and self-loathing that accompanied these thoughts, Hans couldn't deny the pull they had on him. The darkness offered a perverse comfort, a way to escape the overwhelming sense of failure that plagued him.

As he lay there, lost in his fantasies, he knew he was teetering on the edge of an unknown darkness, and he wasn't sure he wanted to step back. The path ahead was dark and dangerous, but it promised a form of control he hadn't felt in a long time, and in his desperation, he was willing to grasp at anything to feel powerful again.

The dark desires were taking over Hans, and he was aware of that.

CHAPTER 4

Breaking Free

The Keller household had become a battlefield, the once beautiful home now regularly echoing with the sounds of bitter arguments and hurtful exchanges. The love that had once bound Hans and Anna together had twisted into a pale shadow of their former intimacy, with each person seeking to hurt the other in a desperate bid for control and revenge.

It started with small, subtle acts of domestic cruelty. Anna would make cutting remarks about Hans's failed career, her words dripping with contempt. "Another rejection letter, Hans? Maybe it's time to face reality. Your glory days are over." The sting of her words was sharp, and Hans could see the satisfaction in her eyes as the punch landed.

Hans retaliated by belittling Anna's social life, mocking the people she spent her time with. "Your gallery might be successful, but it's just a distraction, isn't it? Surrounding yourself with shallow people does make you happy, Anna." His tone was cold, and he revelled in the signs of hurt that crossed her face.

Their fights became more frequent and intense, each one a battle for dominance. They found twisted pleasure in humiliating each other, their words and actions designed to inflict maximum pain. Hans would go through Anna's personal belongings, looking for anything he could use against her. He would bring up her past relationships, questioning her loyalty and integrity.

Anna, in turn, would criticise Hans's appearance, his dwindling social connections, and his drinking habits. She would mock his attempts to write, her words cutting deeper than any physical blow. "Another night with your whiskey and your blank pages, Hans? No wonder you can't write anything worthwhile anymore."

Their fights spilled into every aspect of their domestic life. Mealtimes were fraught with tension, each word a potential spark for another argument. Anna would deliberately cook meals she knew Hans disliked, watching with satisfaction as he forced himself to eat. Hans would leave the house in disarray, knowing it would drive Anna to frustration.

The physical aspect of their relationship grew increasingly perverse and hurtful. What had started as a desperate attempt to reconnect turned into a twisted game of dominance and submission. Their sex life became a battleground, each encounter a mix of pain and pleasure, anger and desire, and to hurt each other physically to the maximum extent possible.

Hans began to push boundaries in the bedroom, his style becoming rough and toxic. He took pleasure in seeing Anna's discomfort and started enjoying the bruises that marked her skin after the sex was over. He enjoyed the power he felt in those moments, in the way he could make her cry out in pain or pleasure, sometimes both. The lines between love and hate, pleasure and pain, became increasingly blurred.

Anna, too, found herself drawn into the darkness. She would provoke Hans, pushing him to the edge, with her actions driven by a need to regain some semblance of control. She discovered that she could wield her power, and her body became a weapon in their twisted dance.

She would bite, scratch, and claw, leaving her own bloodied marks on Hans' skin, which became her form of revenge. She would belittle him if he ejaculated early or took time to harden up, and commented that he had grown old and was maybe becoming impotent.

Their encounters grew more extreme, more violent. Hans would sometimes tie Anna up with his tie. He enjoyed watching her struggle, and her pleas for release fell on his deaf ears. The sight of her bound and helpless naked body stirred something dark within him. He would whisper cruel and vulgar words in her ears while thrusting in and out of her body, his voice a mix of desire and contempt. Her crimson cheeks, filled with her shame, guilt, and humiliation, gave him perverse satisfaction.

Anna found herself both shockingly aroused and repelled by these encounters. Her physical pain was a stark reminder of their fractured relationship, but there was a perverse satisfaction in the intensity of their interactions. She began to enjoy the bruises and the marks that showed she had fought back. The physical pain became a distraction from the emotional agony, a way to feel something, anything, in the numbness that had enveloped her life.

Their home became a twisted sanctuary for their perverse acts. The bedroom, once a place of love and intimacy, was now a stage for their darkest fantasies. The nights were filled with the sounds of their bodies colliding, their moans and cries, and a recurring symphony of pain and pleasure. Each encounter left them both feeling more emotionally broken, more lost, but unable to stop.

Hans's fantasies grew darker and more detailed. He began to imagine others as a part of his twisted roleplays, though he never acted on these thoughts. The idea of humiliating Anna in front of an audience, of making her submit to him while others watched, was a recurring theme in his mind. He knew it was wrong, that it would only deepen the chasm between them, but the dark desire in his mind was a powerful force.

Anna, too, found her thoughts drifting to darker places. She considered having an affair, using another man to hurt Hans as deeply as he had hurt her. The memory of Lukas' tenderness haunted her, a stark contrast to the brutality she now endured. She toyed with the idea of reaching out to him, but could not muster enough courage.

Anna lay in bed, her thoughts drifting to her young intern, Arjun. She had noticed the way his eyes lingered on her, the eager willingness in his every action. The idea of having someone so devoted to her whims was tantalising to her. She toyed with the notion of granting him some liberties, of testing the boundaries of his devotion. Anna's mind wandered to perverse fantasies, where Arjun became her willing servant, while bending to her every desire.

She imagined Arjun at her feet, licking her toes with a mix of reverence and desire, while becoming completely subservient to her. The thought of having such power over him, of moulding him into her private sex slave, excited her in a way she hadn't felt in years. Anna's thoughts grew darker, revelling in the control she could exert, the pleasure she could derive from Arjun's imaginary submission. It was a twisted game, one that filled her with a sense of forbidden thrill, as she imagined the extent of Arjun's obedience and her insatiable desires.

Hans and Anna's mutual destruction became a routine, a sick bedroom dance that neither could escape. They would go through the motions of their daily lives, the tension between them a constant undercurrent, while waiting eagerly for their nightly encounters, when they could hurt each other in their bedroom's darkness.

Friends and acquaintances began to notice the changes, the way they interacted with each other. The once vibrant and loving couple was now becoming a cautionary tale, a reminder of how deep love could also turn to strong hate.

One evening, after another vicious fight, Hans found himself standing on the balcony, staring out at the city lights. The anger and frustration that had driven him for so long now felt hollow. He thought about the man he used to be, the love he used to feel for Anna. The frustrations that had consumed him seemed insurmountable, and he wondered if there was any way back.

Inside, Anna stood in front of the mirror, examining the bruises and marks that covered her body after tonight's roleplay. She felt a twisted sense of pride and shame, the pain a reminder of their perverse connection. She thought about leaving Hans, about starting over, but the idea seemed impossible. The life she had built with Hans, however twisted, was all she had in Zurich.

Their paths had diverged so far from the love they once shared, and yet they were bound together by their mutual destruction. The nights of hurtful, revengeful sex were a manifestation of their deepest fears and insecurities, a way to lash out at each other and themselves. They had become addicted to the cycle of pain and pleasure, unable to find a way out.

As the winds raged outside, the Keller household remained a battleground, each day a new chapter in their spiral of destruction. The love that had once been their anchor was now a distant memory, replaced by a darkness that threatened to consume them both.

The question of whether they could ever find their way back to each other, or if they were doomed to continue their twisted lives forever.

At times, Anna's thoughts began to drift to even darker places. In her moments of deepest resentment, she fantasised about seducing random men on Zurich's streets, not just for her own pleasure, but as a means to utterly destroy Hans. The idea of sleeping with others, particularly men within their social circle, took root in her mind.

She imagined the look of devastation on Hans's face if he were to discover her infidelities, the way it would shatter his already fragile ego and tarnish his reputation. The thought of him knowing that she had found solace and satisfaction in the arms of other men, men who admired and desired her, was a perverse form of revenge that excited her.

Anna envisioned orchestrating sexual encounters at parties and gallery openings, making deliberate choices that would ensure that word of her infidelities would get back to Hans. The humiliation he would feel, the social destruction it would cause for him, fed her darkest desires. She wanted to see him suffer, to feel the same helplessness and betrayal that had consumed her.

The very thought of his friends whispering behind his back, knowing he had been cuckolded, brought a twisted satisfaction that was as intoxicating as it was dangerous. As she plotted these imaginary scenarios, the line between revenge and self-destruction blurred, driving her deeper into a cycle of revenge and despair.

One evening, after yet another brutal fight with Hans, Anna decided to attend an art gala alone. The event was held at a luxurious venue, filled with Zurich's elite, the air buzzing with excitement and creativity. She needed a distraction, a break from the toxicity that had enveloped her life.

As she wandered through the gallery, admiring the exquisite artworks on display, she felt a familiar presence. Lukas. Their eyes met across the room, and Anna felt a jolt of recognition and longing. He smiled warmly and made his way over to her, his presence a soothing balm to her wounded soul.

"Anna, it's been too long," Lukas said, his voice filled with genuine warmth.

"Indeed it has," she replied, her heart fluttering in his presence.

They spent the evening talking, the conversation flowing effortlessly. Lukas was attentive and charming, his laughter infectious. The memory of their previous encounter hung between them, a tantalising reminder of what could have been. As the night progressed, the connection between them grew stronger, and the chemistry was undeniable.

At the end of the evening, Lukas invited Anna back to his studio, and she accepted without hesitation. The studio was a haven of creativity, filled with his paintings and sketches, and the air thick with anticipation of the evening ahead. Lukas poured them both a glass of wine, and they sat on a plush sofa, the atmosphere intimate and charged with sexual chemistry.

As they talked, Lukas gently brushed a strand of hair from Anna's face, his touch sending a shiver down her spine. He leaned in slowly, giving her ample time to pull away, but she didn't. Their lips met in a tender kiss, the softness a stark contrast to the brutality she had endured with Hans. The kiss deepened, their bodies moving closer, the warmth of Lukas's touch enveloping her.

Lukas treated Anna with a tenderness she hadn't experienced in years. As they moved to the bedroom, his touch was deliberate and gentle, as if he were handling a precious piece of art. He took his time undressing her, each piece of clothing removed with a soft, reverent touch that sent shivers down her spine. His hands glided over her skin, warm and soothing, erasing the bruises left by Hans's roughness with every caress. Lukas's eyes held a softness that melted her defences, and for the first time in a long time, Anna felt truly cherished.

Every movement Lukas made was slow and deliberate. He kissed her neck, trailing down to her shoulders, his lips leaving a trail of warmth that contrasted sharply with the cold detachment she had come to expect. His hands roamed her body with an exquisite gentleness, exploring her curves with a patient reverence. Each touch was a question, and he waited for her responses, ensuring she was comfortable and willing. The way he held her, the way he moved, spoke of a deep respect and adoration that made Anna feel safe and valued.

Their lovemaking was passionate yet gentle, a dance of mutual respect and deep affection. Lukas's touch was worshipful, his movements measured and attentive to her every response. He whispered sweet nothings in her ear, his breath warm against her skin, making her feel loved and valued in a way she had not experienced for years.

The contrast to her encounters with Hans was stark. With Hans, the act had been rough and revengeful, filled with anger and desperation. His touch had been harsh, leaving bruises and a lingering sense of violation. But with Lukas, Anna felt safe, adored, and truly seen. The gentleness of his lovemaking was a balm to her wounded soul, and she lost herself in the pleasure of being cherished.

The rhythm of their lovemaking was slow and poetic, a dance of tenderness and passion that brought tears of joy and pleasure to her eyes. She felt her body respond to his, every nerve ending alive with the sensation of being loved and cared for.

Lukas's touch was an exploration of intimacy and connection, far removed from the aggressive encounters she had endured with Hans. He held her close, their bodies entwined in a gentle embrace, his movements unhurried and considerate. He was attuned to her needs, responding to her every sigh and whisper, ensuring she felt nothing but pleasure.

As they reached the depth of their climax together, it was not just a physical release but an emotional one. Anna felt a deep sense of fulfilment and peace, her body and heart both satisfied. In the nakedness of Lukas's arms, she found a sanctuary from the darkness that had plagued her life, a moment of pure, untainted joy that made her believe in the possibility of love and tenderness once again.

As they lay together, Lukas's whispers were filled with admiration and affection. He spoke of her beauty, her strength, and how much he had missed her. His words were like a balm to her wounded spirit, filling her with a warmth she hadn't felt in ages. He took his time, savouring every moment, making her feel like she was the centre of his world.

The experience was transformative for Anna; it was a reminder of what love and intimacy could be, a stark contrast to the pain and humiliation she had grown accustomed to with Hans. In Lukas's arms, she rediscovered a part of herself she thought she had lost forever.

Anna was slowly finding happiness and healing in the romance and thrill of her affair with Lukas.

CHAPTER 5

An Escape to Paradise

In the weeks following their tender encounter, Anna and Lukas found themselves drawn to each other with an intensity that neither could resist. Their meetings became more frequent, each one filled with a sense of adventure and the thrill of newfound love. For Anna, these moments with Lukas were an escape from the toxic environment at home, a chance to feel alive and cherished once again.

Their secret rendezvous began with simple, stolen moments—a coffee date at a quaint café tucked away in the heart of Zurich and a walk along the serene banks of Lake Zurich where they could lose themselves in each other's presence. But as their connection deepened, they sought more privacy, more freedom to explore their feelings without the prying eyes of the city.

Lukas suggested a weekend getaway to the beautiful resort town of Lucerne, nestled at the foot of the Swiss Alps. The idea thrilled Anna, who eagerly created a phoney excuse about an art acquisition trip to go for this trip.

Hans, lost in his own world of bitterness and frustration, barely questioned her plans. With a sense of exhilaration, Anna packed her bags and set off with Lukas for a few days of blissful escape.

Lucerne welcomed them with its charm of a bustling resort town, its cobblestone streets winding through centuries-old buildings adorned with colourful frescoes. They checked into a cosy, intimate resort that overlooked the tranquil waters of Lake Lucerne, with the majestic peaks of Mount Pilatus providing a stunning backdrop. The room was warm and inviting, with a large window that framed the breathtaking view perfectly.

Their days were filled with exploration and wonder. They visited the iconic Chapel Bridge, its wooden structure a blend of history and beauty. Hand in hand, they strolled through the flower-adorned walkways, their laughter mingling with the gentle murmur of the Reuss River below. They wandered through the Old Town, marvelling at the old architecture and the vibrant market stalls that lined the streets.

One afternoon, they took a boat ride across the shimmering Lucerne lake, the cool breeze ruffling their hair as they leaned into each other, sharing whispers and kisses like lovers. Lukas held Anna close, his arms wrapped around her as they gazed at the stunning scenery. The mountains rose majestically around them, their snow-capped peaks reflected in the crystal-clear waters. It felt like a dream, a world away from the turmoil of their everyday lives.

In the evenings, they dined at charming restaurants, savouring Swiss delicacies and sharing intimate conversations. They discovered a mutual love for fine wine, spending hours sampling different varieties and toasting to their budding romance. Each meal was an opportunity to learn more about each other, to share their hopes and dreams, and to deepen the bond that had brought them together.

Back at the resort, their nights were filled with passionate and tender lovemaking. Lukas made love to Anna with the same gentle reverence he had shown before, his touch slow and deliberate, his kisses a promise of devotion. They would lie in bed, wrapped in each other's arms, talking late into the night. The intimacy they shared was a stark contrast to the bitterness and anger that had defined Anna's relationship with Hans.

One morning, they decided to take a hike up Mount Pilatus. The journey was challenging but exhilarating, each step bringing them closer to the summit and to each other. They laughed and teased, their playful banter echoing through the mountain air. At the top, they were rewarded with a panoramic view that took their breath away. They stood together, the world spread out before them, and for a moment, everything else faded away.

Lukas pulled Anna close, his eyes reflecting the awe and love he felt. "This is perfect," he whispered, his voice filled with emotion. "Being here with you, it's like nothing else matters."

Anna smiled, tears of joy glistening in her eyes. "I feel the same way," she replied, her heart full. "I've never felt so alive, so free."

As they embraced each other, with the wind whispering around them, Anna knew that this was the turning point. The love she felt for Lukas was real and profound, a stark contrast to the hollow existence she had left behind. She felt a renewed sense of hope, a belief that happiness was still possible, even in the midst of chaos.

Their weekend in Lucerne was a brief respite from reality, but it strengthened their bond and gave Anna the courage to face the future. She knew that their journey was far from over, but with Lukas by her side, she felt ready to navigate the challenges ahead. Their love was a beacon of light, guiding them through the darkness and promising a brighter tomorrow.

As they returned to Zurich, Anna felt a renewed sense of purpose. She was determined to reclaim her life, and to fight for the happiness she deserved. With Lukas's support, she knew she could overcome the obstacles that lay ahead. Their romance was just beginning, a beautiful escape that held the promise of a better future.

And so, with their hearts full and their spirits high, Anna and Lukas faced the world together, ready to embrace whatever challenges came their way. Their love was a sanctuary, a place where they could find solace and joy, and it was in each other's arms that they discovered the true meaning of happiness.

Lukas had a natural charm that made Anna feel like the most cherished person in the world. He had a way of looking at her, with eyes full of admiration and warmth, that made her heart flutter. Every touch, every word was filled with genuine affection, and he seemed to know exactly how to make her feel special.

He took great care in planning their moments together, always thinking of ways to surprise and delight her. One evening, Lukas arranged a private dinner for them at a secluded spot by Lake Zurich. As the sun set, casting a golden glow over the water, they sat at a table adorned with candles and flowers, the gentle lapping of the waves creating a serene ambiance. Lukas had personally selected her favourite dishes and paired them with a fine Swiss wine, ensuring that every detail was perfect.

As they dined, Lukas's attentiveness made Anna feel adored. He listened intently to her, his eyes never leaving hers, and his genuine interest in her thoughts and feelings made her feel truly understood. They laughed and shared stories, the conversation flowing effortlessly, a testament to the deep connection they had formed.

After dinner, they strolled along the lakeshore, hand in hand, the cool evening air refreshing and invigorating. Lukas stopped suddenly, pulling Anna into his arms and kissing her softly. The kiss was tender and slow, filled with a promise of love and devotion. Anna felt herself melting into him, the world around them fading away as they shared this intimate moment.

Lukas's romantic gestures weren't limited to grand gestures; he also excelled at the small, thoughtful actions that showed how much he cared. He would leave little notes for Anna to find, each one a sweet reminder of his love. A simple "Thinking of you" or "Can't wait to see you tonight" written on a piece of paper would brighten her day and make her heart swell with happiness.

He often surprised her with flowers, not just on special occasions but whenever he felt like making her smile. Lukas knew her favourite blooms and would bring her bouquets of fragrant roses, delicate lilies, or vibrant tulips, each one carefully selected to convey his feelings. These small acts of kindness and thoughtfulness were constant reminders of the depth of his affection.

Lukas also had a playful side that Anna adored. He would plan spontaneous adventures, whisking her away on impromptu trips to explore the beautiful Swiss countryside. They would hike through lush forests, discover hidden waterfalls, and picnic in idyllic meadows, their laughter echoing through the tranquil landscape. These moments of joy and spontaneity brought a sense of freedom and excitement to Anna's life, a stark contrast to the rigidity and tension she had experienced with Hans.

In Lukas's arms, Anna found a sanctuary. His love was a gentle, healing force that soothed her soul and rekindled her spirit. The way he romanced her, with a perfect blend of passion, tenderness, and playfulness, made her feel like she was living in a dream. Each day with Lukas was a new adventure, a beautiful escape from the darkness that had once consumed her life.

Anna and Lukas soon planned another getaway to a secluded villa nestled in the Swiss countryside. The villa, built on the edge of a beautiful lake, had a stunning infinity pool that overlooked the blue waters of the lake. It was the perfect place for them to escape the chaos of their lives and lose themselves in each other.

On their second day at the villa, after a leisurely breakfast on the terrace, Lukas suggested they go for a swim. Anna agreed eagerly, thrilled at the prospect of spending a carefree day in the sun with him. They changed into their swimsuits and made their way to the pool, the warm summer sun casting a golden glow over the water.

The pool was an oasis of calm, the water sparkling invitingly. Lukas was the first to dive in, slicing through the water with effortless grace. Anna followed, feeling the cool water envelop her body as she swam slowly towards him. They played and splashed like carefree children, their laughter echoing around the villa. It was a moment of pure joy, free from the worries that had plagued them for so long.

As the afternoon wore on, the playfulness between them shifted to something more intimate. Lukas swam up behind Anna, wrapping his arms around her waist and pulling her close. She turned in his embrace, their faces just inches apart. The look in his eyes was one of deep affection and carnal desire, and it made her heart race.

He kissed her softly at first, his lips brushing against hers with a tenderness that took her breath away. The kiss deepened, becoming more passionate as their wet tongues played together and they explored each other's mouth deeply. Lukas's hands roamed around her back, tracing the curves of her body with a touch that was both gentle and hungry.

With a playful glint in his eye, Lukas lifted Anna effortlessly, guiding her to the edge of the pool where she could sit on the edge with her feet still submerged in the pool's water. He positioned his body between her shapely thighs, gently pushed them wider, while his hands were caressing her breasts as he leaned in to kiss her wet mouth.

The sensation of his hard manhood against her wet body, combined with the warmth of the sun and the coolness of the water, was intoxicating for Anna. A slow and sexy moan escaped Anna's lips as Lukas' manhood entered her slowly, moving with a deliberate, sweet rhythm that sent throngs of pleasure through her body.

Their lovemaking was slow and passionate, every touch and kiss filled with a sense of reverence and desire. Lukas took his time, his hard manhood filling her eager crevice with an animal passion that made Anna feel worshipped. He whispered words of love, lust and admiration, his voice a soothing balm to her soul. The way he looked at her, with eyes full of adoration, made her feel like the most beautiful woman in the world.

As they moved together in pleasure, the pool water created a gentle rhythm around them. Anna felt a profound connection with Lukas. It was as if their beautiful bodies and souls were in perfect harmony, each thrust bringing them closer together. The pleasurable sensations were heightened by the cold water around them, each wave sending ripples of pleasure through their body.

Anna's climax built slowly and strongly, a wave of mind-boggling ecstasy that started deep within her and radiated outwards. When she finally came, it was unlike anything she had ever experienced. She moaned loudly, her hands gripping Lukas's shoulders with her nails deep in his flesh, as her body trembled with the intensity of her carnal release.

Lukas followed soon after, his own pleasure evident in the way he held her tightly, his face buried in her luscious bosom and lips firmly caressing her taut nipples. From the depths of their throats came loud primal cries, as they reached their pleasure peaks again and again, flooding each other with waves of passion.

They stayed like that for a while, wrapped in each other's arms, the cold water gently lapping around them. The world seemed to stand still, and in that moment, nothing else mattered. It was the best sex Anna had ever had, not just because of the physical sensations, but because of the deep emotional connection she felt with Lukas.

As the sun began to set, casting a warm glow over the pool, they finally pulled apart, their bodies still tingling from the experience. Lukas helped Anna back into the water, and they swam together, savouring the peacefulness of the moment. When they finally emerged from the pool, they wrapped themselves in towels and sat on the edge, watching the sun dip below the horizon.

Anna leaned her head on Lukas's shoulder, feeling a sense of contentment she hadn't known in years. "I love you," she whispered, her voice filled with emotion.

Lukas kissed the top of her head, his arm wrapped around her protectively. "I love you too, Anna," he replied softly. "More than you'll ever know."

In that idyllic Swiss setting, with the stars beginning to twinkle in the sky above them, Anna knew that she had found something truly special with Lukas. Their love was a sanctuary, a place where she could heal and grow. And as they sat together, bathed in the soft glow of the fading light, she was ready to embrace whatever the future held for them.

Anna felt hopeful for the first time in a really long time.

CHAPTER 6

Return to the Darkness

The happy days spent with Lukas felt like a dream to Anna. It was a rare escape from the harsh reality of her life with Hans. As she drove back to Zurich, her heart ached with longing for the gentle touch and tender words of Lukas, who had made her feel cherished and alive.

But now, she had to return to the suffocating atmosphere of her marriage with Hans, where resentment and anger lurked around every corner.

When Anna walked through the door of their home, Hans was waiting. The familiar scent of whiskey hung in the air, and the living room was dimly lit, casting long shadows that seemed to mirror the darkness in their relationship. Hans looked up as she entered, his eyes narrowing with suspicion and bitterness.

"Where have you been?" he demanded, his voice slurred slightly from the alcohol.

"Art acquisition trip," Anna replied curtly, avoiding his gaze. She moved to put her bags down, but Hans was already on his feet, blocking her path.

"Don't lie to me, Anna. I know you've been with someone else," he hissed, his breath hot and reeking of liquor.

She met his eyes, defiance flickering in her green irises. "And what if I have been? What do you care, Hans? You're too busy drowning in your own misery to notice anything else."

Hans's face twisted with rage, and for a moment, Anna thought he might strike her. Instead, he grabbed her arm roughly, pulling her close. "You're still my wife," he growled. "And you're coming to bed with me tonight."

Anna wrenched her arm free, her skin burning where his fingers had dug in. "No, Hans. I'm not doing this anymore. I'm not your punching bag."

But Hans was relentless. He grabbed her again, this time with more force, dragging her towards the bedroom. Anna struggled, her resistance only fueling his anger. They stumbled into the room, their bodies colliding with the furniture in a chaotic act of fury and hatred.

Hans pushed Anna onto the bed, his eyes dark with a mix of desire and hatred. "You don't get to refuse me," he spat, his hands tearing at her clothes with a brutal intensity. Anna fought back, her nails raking across his skin, but Hans was stronger, his rage giving him a terrifying strength.

Her clothes were soon torn away, and Hans pinned Anna beneath him. His breath was furious and harsh. "You want this," he insisted, his voice appearing as a low, menacing growl. "You want me."

Anna's eyes blazed with defiance. "I don't want you, Hans, I hate you. You are a disgusting loser!"

Hans's rage reached a fever pitch, and in his twisted state of mind, he sought to assert his control through violence. As Anna lay beneath him, her defiance only seemed to fuel his anger. He raised his hand and slapped her hard across the face, the sharp crack of the slap echoing through the room. Anna's head snapped to the side, and a cry of pain escaped her lips.

"Look at me," Hans demanded, his voice a low, menacing growl. "Look at me while I do this to you."

Tears streamed down Anna's cheeks as she turned her head back to face him, her eyes filled with a mix of fear and loathing. The slap left a burning sting on her cheek, but it was the cruelty in his eyes that cut the deepest. Hans's hand gripped her chin roughly, forcing her to maintain eye contact as he continued his sexual assault.

He entered her roughly, with no foreplay whatsoever. The brutal entry of Hans' manhood caused a tearing pain through Anna's body. Her eyes boiled over with agony, and Hans covered her mouth with his burly palms to stop her struggle, as he shoved and thrust inside her like a dog in heat.

With each deeper thrust, Hans's grip tightened, his fingers digging painfully into her bosom's flesh. He slapped her again, this time harder, leaving a crimson mark that quickly began to bruise. Anna started sobbing, her body shaking with each painful thrust. The tears flowed freely now, a manifestation of her profound agony and helplessness.

"Stop crying, you are enjoying this," Hans barked, his voice laced with sarcasm and fury. "Stop acting like a goddamn victim, and be the whore you actually are."

But Anna couldn't stop crying. The pain and humiliation, both physical and emotional, was overwhelming. She felt her spirit breaking under the weight of his brutality. Hans's actions were devoid of any tenderness or love; they were purely driven by a need to dominate and humiliate. Each slap, each violent thrust, each vulgar word was a reminder of how far they had fallen, how twisted their relationship had become.

As he continued, Hans's thrusts grew increasingly frantic, his sex became more punishing. Multiple slaps landed on Anna's cheeks with escalating violence, leaving a trail of crimson across Anna's cheeks and left her lips swollen.

He choked her throat at will, only leaving it when her eyes boiled over and she started gasping for breath. He twisted her taut nipples mercilessly and bit her breasts like a hungry wolf, eager for his pound of flesh. He spat at her face, while he rode her bruised labia, punishing her in a never before animalistic manner.

Pleasure and sadism intertwined in his mind, creating a euphoric high. This was unlike anything he had ever experienced. In those moments, he felt a twisted sense of power, reminiscent of his former glory when he was successful and on top of the world.

Anna's helplessness, pain and agony beneath his harsh masculine force sent waves of dark sadistic pleasure through him. The sounds of her cries, the sight of her battered beautiful body, and the intoxicating power trip consumed him in totality.

He was oblivious to everything else, lost in a perverse pleasure that became his only guiding force. Hans moaned loudly, while he ravaged Anna with unseen animalistic fury. His actions were driven by a need to completely dominate and destroy her. In this darkness of the bedroom, he felt invincible, a god of his own twisted creation.

Anna's sobs grew louder, her cries of agony, pain and shame echoing through the room. She felt completely powerless, trapped in a long nightmare from which there was no escape.

The bed creaked and groaned under the strain of their violent encounter, the stain covered sheets a tangled mess around them. Hans's hands roamed her body with a roughness that made her skin crawl, and his touch akin to an assault on her tender frame.

He whispered cruel, insulting and deeply degrading things in her ear, his voice a twisted parody of the loving whispers she had once known from Hans.

Anna's sobs became quieter, the pain and humiliation leaving her numb and detached. She closed her eyes, trying to block out the reality of what was happening, but the sounds, smells and sensations were inescapable. The tears continued to flow silently, her body shaking with each harsh thrust and each slap that landed on her already bruised face.

She closed her eyes, trying to detach herself from the nightmare unfolding on top of her. She thought of Lukas, of the gentle way he had touched her, the softness of his kiss. But the memories only made the present more unbearable, a stark contrast to the depravity she was currently enduring.

When it finally ended, Hans let out a loud, deep cry of victorious satisfaction as he came inside her and pulled out with a sharp jerk. He collapsed beside her, his chest heaving from exertion, his lips curling into a perverse smile of triumph.

The room fell into a heavy silence, the air thick with the scent of sweat and anger. Anna lay still, her body aching and bruised, her spirit crushed by the violence and degradation she had endured.

Hans turned his head to look at her, his eyes searching for something he couldn't find. "Are you satisfied, Anna?" he asked bitterly, his voice hoarse and sarcastic.

Anna didn't respond. She couldn't bring herself to speak, to acknowledge the horror of what had just happened. She felt a deep, consuming emptiness, a void where her love for Hans had once been.

Hans reached out, his hand trembling, but Anna recoiled, the touch sending a shiver of revulsion through her body. "Don't touch me," she whispered, her voice filled with a cold, cutting finality.

He withdrew his hand, his face contorted with a mix of anger and hate. "Fine," he muttered, turning away from her. "We're done here."

Anna lay on the bed, staring at the ceiling, the darkness of the room closing in around her. She felt trapped, suffocated by the weight of their failed marriage. The forced sexual encounter had left her feeling violated and hollow, her body and soul scarred by the violence and brutality that had consumed her completely.

As the first light of dawn began to filter through the curtains, Anna made a silent vow to herself. She would find a way to escape this nightmare, to reclaim her life and her dignity. The road ahead would be long and difficult, but she was determined to find her way back to the light, away from the darkness that had engulfed her.

With a heavy heart and a steely resolve, Anna rose from the bed, leaving Hans and the remnants of their shattered relationship behind. She had taken the first step towards her own happiness.

Anna knew that she would never look back.

CHAPTER 7

The Young Lover

Anna sat in the dimly lit living room, her thoughts swirling with confusion and resolve. The divorce papers were still tucked away in her drawer, a silent reminder of the decision she had yet to make.

She was still living with Hans, but their relationship was hanging by a thread. Her heart ached for Lukas, the man who had shown her what true love and tenderness could be, but the realities of life kept her hanging to a situation that had long since become unbearable.

Lukas, despite his deep love for Anna, was not financially independent.

He was an artist, still struggling to make a name for himself. The thought of leaving Hans and starting a new life with Lukas was intoxicating, but it was also fraught with uncertainty. Anna knew that if she left now, it would place an immense burden on Lukas, and she couldn't bear the thought of that. So she stayed, biding her time, waiting for the right moment.

Hans saw the growing distance between them. He could see the way Anna's eyes would light up when she spoke of her art gallery or the way she seemed to come alive when she thought he wasn't watching. He suspected she was thinking of leaving him, and the thought filled him with a mix of dread and rage. Unable to confront her directly, he resorted to following her, trying to uncover the truth of her intentions.

One afternoon, Hans decided to secretly follow Anna to the gallery. He watched from a distance as she interacted with clients and colleagues, her demeanour vibrant and alive. It was a stark contrast to the cold, detached woman she had become at home. He saw the way her eyes sparkled when she received a message on her phone, her smile revealing a hidden world of happiness that he was no longer a part of.

His suspicions were confirmed when he saw Anna leave the gallery later that evening. She walked briskly, her steps light with purpose. Hans trailed her, careful to stay out of sight. She made her way to a small cafe tucked away on a quiet street. Hans watched from across the road as she entered, his heart pounding with a mix of jealousy and fear.

Inside the cafe, Anna found Lukas waiting for her. His face lit up as she approached, and he stood to embrace her with a gentle kiss to her lips. They sat together, their heads close, talking in hushed tones. Hans couldn't hear their conversation, but he could see the tenderness in their gestures, the way Lukas held her hand and the way Anna leaned into him.

Hans stood outside the cafe, hidden in the shadows, his eyes followed Anna as she met Lukas inside. The sight of her with a much younger, handsome man ignited a fierce jealousy within him. He watched through the glass as Anna's face lit up with a smile, her reddish-brown hair glowing in the soft light of the cafe, as she kissed Lukas back and smiled at him tenderly. Lukas also leaned in, with his touch lingering on Anna's arm, and his gaze full of admiration and desire.

Hans' fists clenched at his sides, knuckles white with suppressed fury, as he observed the intimate gestures—the light brush of fingers, the shared laughter, the way their eyes met and lingered.

Each affectionate moment between them felt like a dagger to Hans' heart, a brutal reminder of the love and passion that had slipped away from his own life. The scene before him, filled with warmth and connection, only fueled his dark, consuming jealousy, leaving him seething with a mix of anger and despair.

The sight was a knife to his heart. Hans had always known, deep down, that he was losing her, but seeing it so plainly was almost too much to bear. He turned away, his mind racing with thoughts of betrayal and revenge. He couldn't stand the thought of Anna finding happiness with a much younger man, and the anger and jealousy that simmered within him began to boil over.

Hans returned home alone, the silence of the house pressing down on him like a suffocating weight. He walked through the dimly lit hallway, his footsteps echoing off the walls, and made his way to his study room.

The room, once a sanctuary of creativity and success, now felt like a prison filled with the ghosts of his past achievements. He sank into his worn leather chair, his mind replaying the scene at the cafe over and over again—the image of Anna with Lukas, the younger man who seemed to embody everything Hans was not.

His thoughts spiralled, a chaotic whirlwind of jealousy, anger, and despair. He couldn't escape the gnawing sense of failure that had come to define his life. His writing had stalled, rejected manuscripts piled high on his desk, which mocked his ability as a writer.

Anna's success with her gallery was a constant reminder of what he had lost, with each accolade that she received twisting the knife deeper in Hans' heart. And now, to see her finding solace and passion with someone younger, someone who looked at her the way he used to—it was more than he could bear.

Hans's mind raced, searching desperately for a solution, for some way to regain control of his life and his relationship. But every thought led to a dead end, every plan crumbled under the weight of reality.

As Hans sat in his study, sipping his brand of cheap whiskey, his mind spiralled. He envisioned the worst-case scenarios with vivid, torturous clarity. In his mind's eye, he saw Anna in Lukas's bed, their bodies entwined in passionate embrace, her laughter and sighs of pleasure filling the room.

The thought of Lukas's youthful hands exploring Anna's luscious and supple body, and Anna giving him sexual responses she hadn't given Hans in years, was a torment that was eating his soul. He could almost hear their whispered conversations, their shared intimacy and pleasurable moans, a cruel reminder of what he had lost.

His thoughts then drifted to Arjun, the young intern who followed Anna around like a devoted puppy. Hans imagined Arjun eagerly fulfilling Anna's every demand, ready to please her in ways Hans felt he no longer could.

The image of Anna lying with Arjun in a secret hotel room, her eyes closed in ecstasy as the young boy worshipped her naked body, was unbearable. Hans's writer's imagination ran wild, picturing Anna with every young man on Zurich's streets.

The more he drank, the more the boundaries between reality and his darkest fantasies blurred, leaving him on the brink of losing his sanity entirely.

With his bottle of whiskey emptied and his glass discarded on the floor, Hans struggled to get up. The study, filled with relics of his past success, felt like a tomb. He gripped the edges of his desk, his knuckles white with rage, with frustration and helplessness washed over him.

His failures loomed large, suffocating him, and the image of Anna's happiness with another man was a torment he couldn't escape.

With this new information, the tension between them grew even more palpable. Hans's suspicions fueled his anger, and he became increasingly erratic. He would question Anna about her day, his tone laced with accusation, but she would deflect, maintaining a calm facade that only seemed to infuriate him more.

One evening, after another strained dinner, Hans confronted Anna in the living room. "Who were you with today?" he demanded, his voice shaking with barely controlled rage.

Anna looked up from her book, her expression calm but wary. "I was at the gallery, Hans. Where else would I be?"

"Don't lie to me!" he shouted, stepping closer. "I saw you at the Franzos cafe in District 4. Who was he?"

Anna's heart raced, but she kept her voice steady. "It's none of your business, Hans. We haven't been a real couple for a long time. You know that."

His face contorted with anger, and he grabbed her arm, pulling her to her feet. "You are my wife, Anna. You do not get to walk away that easily," he said, chewing each word.

She pulled away, her eyes blazing with defiance. "I may be your wife on paper, but that's all. You lost me a long time ago, Hans. I've found someone who treats me with the love and respect I deserve."

The words hit him like a blow to his face, and for a moment, Hans was speechless. Then, in a fit of rage, he raised his hand and slapped her hard across the face. Anna stumbled back, her cheek burning from the impact, a single drop of blood forming at her nose. She looked at him, tears of anger and hatred streaming down her face.

"I hate you," she hissed back, her voice filled with a mix of hate and determination. "I loathe the animal that you have become."

Hans's anger evaporated, replaced by a crushing sense of regret and despair. He reached out, but Anna recoiled, her eyes filled with a loathing that cut him to the core. She turned and fled to the bedroom, slamming the door behind her.

Hans stood alone in the living room, his heart pounding. He couldn't lose her, but he didn't know how to hold on to her either. The realisation that Anna was slipping away, that she had found solace in the arms of another younger man, left him feeling hollow and desperate. He knew he had to change, but the darkness within him was a formidable foe.

Meanwhile, Anna lay on the bed, her body trembling with a mix of fear and anger. The encounter had shaken her, but it had also solidified her resolve. She couldn't continue living this way, trapped in a loveless marriage with a man who had become a stranger. She had to find a way out, to break free and start her life afresh with Lukas.

In the days that followed, Anna began to make plans. She secretly met with a lawyer, discussing her options and laying the groundwork for her escape. Each meeting with Lukas was a balm to her wounded spirit, his love and support giving her the strength she needed to move forward.

Hans continued to watch her, his paranoia growing with each passing day. He couldn't bear the thought of losing her, but he didn't know how to win her back.

One evening, as Anna prepared to leave for another secret meeting with Lukas, Hans cornered her in the hallway. "I know you're planning something," he said, his voice low and dangerous. "But you won't get away with it. You are mine, Anna."

She looked at him, her eyes filled with determination. "Not for much longer, Hans. I am done living in fear. I am done being your prisoner. I am leaving, and there is nothing you can do to stop me.

With those words, Anna walked out the door, leaving Hans standing in the hallway, his heart pounding with a mix of rage and despair.

CHAPTER 8
The Sinister Plan

Hans sat alone in his dimly lit study room, the familiar scent of whiskey and stale smoke thick in the air. The divorce papers that he found hidden in Anna's drawers lay crumpled in front of him, a stark reminder of the life that was slipping through his fingers.

He had spent countless hours trying to figure out how to stop Anna from leaving him, but each option seemed more futile than the last.

At first, he considered begging for her forgiveness, promising to change himself and make amends. He imagined falling to his knees in front of Anna, tears streaming down his face as he begs for another chance.

But deep down, he knew it was too late for that. Anna had moved on, her heart now belonging to Lukas.

Hans's financial situation was also growing increasingly dire. His writing, once celebrated and lucrative, had failed to produce successful works in recent years. With each rejected manuscript, his savings dwindled.

Living in Zurich, one of the most expensive cities in the world, only increased his financial struggles. The cost of maintaining their lifestyle was immense, and he was struggling to keep up with the bills.

The looming possibility of Anna leaving him added a layer of desperation. She was running one of the most successful art galleries in Zurich and without her financial support, he would be unable to afford even the basic necessities in the expensive city of Zurich. The fear of losing everything weighed heavily on him, adding to his mounting stress and anxiety.

Desperation gnawed at Hans as his world seemed to crumble around him. The image of Anna and Lukas together was an unrelenting torture. He then contemplated sabotaging Anna's relationship with Lukas. Perhaps if he could expose some flaw or secret, Anna would realise Lukas wasn't the man she thought he was.

Determined to find something—anything—that could sever the bond between Anna and her younger lover, Hans decided to hire a private detective.

He scoured the city for a discreet and ruthless detective, and found a seasoned investigator. With a hefty advance payment that he could barely afford, Hans set the detective on Lukas's trail. He instructed the detective to dig up every dirty detail on Lukas, no matter how insignificant, hoping to find some evidence against Lukas.

As the days dragged on, Hans's anxiety grew, his mind racing with fantasies of exposing Lukas and reclaiming Anna. The cost was high, but the potential payoff was worth any price in Hans's mind.

Hans anxiously awaited the detective's report, his heart pounding with a mix of fear and anticipation. When the envelope finally arrived, he tore it open, scanning the pages with desperate eyes.

To his shock, the report on Lukas came back clean. The detective had found nothing suspicious—no hidden secrets, no dark past, and no illicit activities. Lukas was exactly who he appeared to be: a young, charming man with a spotless record. The realisation hit Hans like a punch in the face, leaving him even more clueless and defeated.

Desperation led him to consider more drastic measures. He thought about fleeing, disappearing from Anna's life entirely in the hope that his absence would make her reconsider. But the idea of living as a fugitive, always looking over his shoulder, was too daunting. Moreover, his pride wouldn't allow him to abandon his home and life without a fight.

Hans's mind grew darker with each passing day. He started to entertain thoughts of harming Lukas, removing the man who had stolen Anna from him. But every scenario he conjured seemed too risky, too likely to backfire and leave him with nothing. The fear of getting caught, of spending the rest of his life in prison, was enough to deter him.

As the weeks dragged on, Hans's thoughts turned even more sinister. He began to consider the unthinkable—if he couldn't have Anna, then no one else would. The idea of killing her started as a whisper in the back of his mind, a dark seed planted by his overwhelming despair.

At first, he recoiled from the thought, horrified by the monstrous idea. But as the days passed, the seed took root, growing stronger and more insistent. He thought about the freedom it would bring, and the finality of it. No more sleepless nights, and no more torment. It would be a way to reclaim control, and to end his suffering once and for all.

Hans began to plan meticulously, and his mind got consumed by the intricate details of the plan. He researched methods, looking for a way that would be quick and foolproof. Poison seemed too impersonal, and the idea of a staged accident felt too risky. He wanted to be sure, to see the light fade from her eyes as he carried out his plan.

He started to imagine how he would do it, and the scenarios played out in his mind with chilling clarity. He would wait for the perfect moment, when Anna was alone and unsuspecting. He would confront her, make her understand the depth of his pain, and then he would end her. The thought gave him a twisted sense of peace, a solution to the pain that had consumed him.

In his darkest moments, Hans even convinced himself that he was doing it out of love. He told himself that ending Anna's life would spare her the pain of their failed marriage, and that it was a merciful solution.

But deep down, he knew the truth—it was his last, desperate grasp at control, a final act of revenge against the woman who had torn his world apart.

As he sat in the study, sipping his whiskey, staring at the crumpled divorce papers, Hans made his decision final. The darkness within him had won, pushing him to a place from which there was no return.

He would kill Anna, and in doing so, he would end the nightmare that his life had become. The thought brought a cold, grim resolve to his heart, and he knew there was no turning back.

The decision to kill Anna weighed heavily on Hans' mind, but he knew he couldn't do it alone. He was a lonely drunkard after all.

The thought of reaching out to someone from his past, maybe someone who has the required criminal experience that he needed, began to take shape in Hans' mind. Hans picked up his iPhone and scrolled through his contacts, searching for the names of old friends and acquaintances who had lived on the edge of law and society.

His first call was to Karl, an old schoolmate who had a reputation for being involved in shady dealings. They hadn't spoken in years, but Hans remembered the rumours that went around regarding Karl's activities—gambling, smuggling, and, some whispered, even darker pursuits. Hans's heart pounded as he dialled the number, each ring heightening his anxiety. When Karl finally answered, his voice was rough and cautious.

"Hans? It's been a long time. What do you want?" Karl's tone was devoid of the warmth of old friendships, replaced by a guarded suspicion.

Hans took a deep breath. "Karl, I need your help. I'm in a situation, and I don't know where else to turn." He hesitated, then added, "I need to know if you have any experience...with getting rid of someone."

There was a long pause on the other end of the line. Hans could almost hear the gears turning in Karl's mind. Finally, Karl spoke, his voice low and dangerous. "Hans, you're talking about something serious. Killing someone isn't a joke. Are you sure you know what you're asking?"

Hans swallowed hard, the reality of his request settling heavily on him. "Yes, I know. I am really desperate, Karl. She is ruining my life, and I see no other way out."

Karl sighed, and said, "Meet me tomorrow night at the old warehouse by the docks. We will talk then."

The next day, Hans felt a mix of fear and anticipation as he made his way to the warehouse. He gripped the steering wheel tightly as he navigated through the bustling streets of Zurich, his mind a chaotic storm of dark thoughts and grim determination.

He could hardly appreciate the charming facades of Zurich's buildings or the serene beauty of Lake Zurich as he drove. Each honking car and bustling pedestrian only amplified his sense of urgency and impending doom.

As he steered off the main roads into the narrower, dimly lit lanes, the familiar landmarks of Zurich faded into the background. The journey to the old warehouse felt surreal, like a descent into a dark underworld.

As Hans drove through Zurich's winding streets, his mind drifted between two starkly different realities. On the one hand, he saw his life with Anna, filled with the bitter memories of their deteriorating relationship, and the constant arguments that left him feeling hollow and angry.

He remembered the early days, when Anna's laughter filled their home and their love seemed unbreakable. But those days felt like distant times. The thought of living without her, free from the torment of her presence and her affairs, brought a twisted sense of relief mixed with an undercurrent of fear and loneliness.

In the other reality, Hans imagined a life completely devoid of Anna. The initial sense of liberation quickly gave way to a haunting emptiness. He envisioned the quiet, empty rooms of their home, the absence of her voice, and the absolute silence that would engulf the house.

The idea of being alone, truly alone, gnawed at him, leaving him questioning whether he can bear such isolation. His thoughts oscillated between the two scenarios, neither offering a sense of peace. As he approached the old warehouse, the weight of his decision pressed down on him, intensifying the turmoil within his mind.

Hans's mind raced with thoughts of his deteriorating life and the desperate measures he was about to take. The streets grew quieter, the buildings more industrial, and Hans felt a grim sense of purpose strengthening within him. He knew there was no turning back now and he was committed to seeing his sinister plan through.

The air was thick with the smell of saltwater and decay, the setting sun casting long shadows that seemed to stretch like grasping hands.

Karl stood at the entrance of the old warehouse. Karl had completely transformed into a seasoned professional thug, which was evident in every aspect of his appearance. His face, now marked by deep lines and scars, spoke of a number of tough years he had spent dealing with the underworld.

They stood in the shadow of the warehouse, the distant sounds of the city a mere hum in the background. Hans felt a chill run down his spine as Karl stared at him with a steely gaze. "So, you really want to go through with this?"

Hans nodded, his voice barely above a whisper. "I don't see any other way out, Karl."

Karl nodded his head, tossing his cigarette to the ground and crushing it under his boot. "I still need to warn you once, Hans. You are playing with fire here. This is not something you can just walk away from. Once this game is set up, there's no going back."

Hans clenched his teeth. "I understand, Karl. Now just tell me what I need to do to eliminate her."

Karl looked at him for a long moment, then sighed again. "Alright. I'll give you some names, people who might be able to help. But remember, this is on you. You are the one making this choice. My role is done here."

Hans nodded, accepting the crumpled piece of paper Karl handed him, its surface scribbled with names and numbers in a hasty script. He then passed a small wad of cash to Karl, who smiled slyly, his eyes gleaming with satisfaction.

As Hans tucked the paper into his pocket, he felt the weight of his decision settle even more heavily on his shoulders. The path he was choosing was dark and irreversible, but he was too far away to turn back now.

Hans walked back from his meeting with Karl to the car park. With the names of potential hired killers tucked away in his pocket, a wave of fear swept over him. Every unknown person he passed on the street seemed to look at him with knowing eyes, their gazes piercing through his face and straight into his darkest thoughts.

He could feel their judgement, their silent condemnation, as if they were all aware of the sinister plan taking shape in his mind. The weight of their imaginary scrutiny made his steps falter, each random face in the crowd staring at him, with a haunting reminder of the bottomless pit he was descending into.

Hans's paranoia grew with each step, his mind imagining scenarios where random whispers followed him, and strangers exchanged suspicious glances in his direction. The city around him felt hostile, the familiar streets now alien and foreboding.

Every laugh, every murmur on the street seemed like an accusation, amplifying his sense of impending doom. He held the paper in his pocket, its presence a burning reminder of his guilt and desperation. The once vibrant city of Zurich now felt like a collection of hostile eyes, all watching, all knowing, all silently condemning him for the dark path he had chosen.

With his paranoia running circles around him, he was able to locate the car parking spot with great difficulty. But once inside the safety of his car, he reaffirmed his resolve. Anna would not be allowed to destroy him.

If it all, he would destroy Anna completely, and teach Lukas a painful lesson.

CHAPTER 9

A Night of Debauchery

Hans came out of the docks area, the paper with the contract killer's names and numbers feeling like a heavy weight in his pocket. The conversation with Karl had left him feeling hollow and paranoid.

As he went around aimlessly through the city streets, the neon signs of Zurich's nightlife began to blur into a colourful haze. He needed a drink, something strong to numb the chaos in his mind, if only for a little while.

Hans navigated the narrow lanes of Zurich, slipping through the dimly lit streets of District 5. As he crossed Langstrasse, the atmosphere grew darker, the area well known for its seedy bars and shadowy figures lurking in the dark alleys.

He found himself in front of a seedy bar, its entrance illuminated by a flickering sign. The door creaked as he pushed it open, and the smell of stale beer and perspiration hit him like a wall. Hans made his way to the bar, his eyes scanning the dimly lit room. He ordered a double whiskey, downing it in one go before ordering another. The strong alcohol burned his throat, but it also dulled his thoughts and paranoia.

As the night wore on, Hans's inhibitions melted away with each drink. He lost track of time, the hours blending together in a fog of liquor and tobacco. It was during this haze that he noticed two young women sitting at the end of the bar, their eyes locked onto him with a mix of curiosity and interest.

The first woman, a tall blonde with sharp features and an air of confident seduction, approached him. "You look like you could use some company," she said, her voice smooth and inviting.

Hans glanced up, his vision slightly blurred. "Maybe I do," he replied, his words slurring slightly.

The second woman, a petite brunette with a mischievous smile, joined them. "We're great at making people forget their troubles," she said, leaning in close. "What do you say?"

Hans's judgement was clouded by the alcohol, and the idea of losing himself in the company of these two shady women seemed appealing. "Why not?" he mumbled, gesturing for the bartender to pour more drinks.

The three of them moved to a private booth in the back of the bar. Here the atmosphere was more intimate and the booth provided much needed privacy from the rest of the patrons. Hans continued to drink, his head swimming with a mix of desire and lust. The tall blonde introduced herself as Nadia, and the brunette, named Sofia. Both the girls flanked him, their sensuous bodies pressing against his body in a way that was both comforting and inviting.

The intimacy of the booth allowed Hans to observe the girls in more detail. He liked what he saw.

Nadia stood out with her tall, confident body and striking blonde hair that cascaded down her shoulders. Her sharp, blue eyes sparkled with a mix of allure and cunning, attracting potential customers with a practised ease. She wore a tight, red dress that clung to her curves, accentuating her seductive presence. Her lips, painted a bold crimson, curled into a knowing smile, making it clear she was a master at her trade, luring men into her web with her effortless charm and sensuality.

Sophia, on the other hand, was petite and pretty brunette, with a hesitant demeanour that contrasted sharply with her friend Nadia's bold confidence. Her dark hair framed her delicate face, and her soft brown eyes carried a hint of vulnerability. Dressed in a modest but alluring outfit, she seemed approachable and easily tamed, giving off an air of submissiveness. Her shy smile and tentative gestures suggested she was more comfortable following Nadia's lead in luring customers.

Hans's night in the bar's private booth with Sophia and Nadia started as a whirlwind of excess and indulgence. The three of them were drinking heavily, with Hans's money flowing freely on the most expensive drinks on the menu.

Sophia, with her hesitant charm, and Nadia, with her bold confidence, kept the conversation lively and flirtatious. Hans, fueled by alcohol and lust, found himself lost in their company, momentarily forgetting his troubles. The booth was filled with laughter and the clinking of glasses, a mask of happy revelry masking the darker intentions brewing beneath the surface.

In the private booth of the bar, Hans felt a fleeting sense of comfort as Sophia and Nadia cosily embraced him, their feminine soft bodies igniting a primal response within him. Their soft hands caressed his arms and shoulders, their laughter a soft, seductive melody that drowned out his troubled thoughts.

The girls, seasoned in the art of pleasing customers, expertly played to Hans's weaknesses. Their intimate movements and bold touches designed to make him feel desired and powerful. Hans, enveloped in their lure, momentarily forgot his misery, losing himself in the intoxicating blend of their company and the expensive drinks they continued to order on his tab.

In the dimly lit corner of the Zurich bar, Hans felt an exhilarating rush as the girls allowed him some liberties. Sophia's hesitant, yet willing, demeanour complemented Nadia's confident approach, creating a tantalising contrast. Hans's hands explored the sensual curves of their bodies, with the warmth of their skin igniting a primal satisfaction within him. The girls, masters of their craft, expertly guided his touches, ensuring he remained pleasured by their seductive presence, deepening his intoxication with each passing moment.

As the night progressed and the alcohol loosened inhibitions, Hans's hand began to wander, sliding inside Sophia's dress. She allowed him a fleeting moment of pleasure, while he lustily kneaded her ample bosom, and then firmly pushed him away, with a mischievous glint in her eye.

"That'll cost you extra," she teased, her voice dripping with playful teasing.

Nadia burst into lusty laughter, the sound a sharp contrast to the sultry atmosphere. Hans, momentarily taken aback, couldn't help but grin at the brazen remark. Their interaction, a blend of seduction and commercial reality, deepened the strange allure of the two women.

Hans reached into his wallet, pulling out a rich wad of cash and spilling it extravagantly over the laps of Sophia and Nadia. The girls' eyes lit up with excitement as they eagerly scooped up the money, and their demeanour shifted instantly. With their wallets now richer, they allowed Hans many more liberties with their sensuous bodies.

In the private booth of the bar, away from prying eyes, the atmosphere grew more sexually charged. Hans's hands explored the women's bodies abundantly with the newfound freedom. The girls' boundaries dissolved with each bill they pocketed. The women began their practised, expert moans and sounds to further encourage Hans's drunken debauchery.

The mix of alcohol, money, and forbidden touches created an intoxicating blend that drove Hans deeper into a haze of indulgence and desire. Sophia and Nadia, now more accommodating, leaned in closer, their touches more inviting, their hands getting expertly in Hans' trousers, ensuring that his night was filled with the lusty pleasures he badly craved.

Their tongues mutually entwined and their hands roamed over each other's bodies, melding into a fervent tangle of heaving, breathless intensity. Hans momentarily watched as the girls began to kiss each other, and then he joined in the party with his eager and wet tongue. The air was thick with the sounds of their loud passions and moans, transforming the dark corner of the bar into a secret cave of desire.

As the night deepened, Hans's guard lowered even further. He found himself talking, the words spilling out in a drunken torrent.

"I'm stuck in a nightmare," he confessed, his voice heavy with emotion. "My wife... she's destroying me. I can't take it anymore."

Nadia's eyes glittered with interest. "What are you going to do about it?" she asked, her hand resting on the insides of his thigh, gently caressing his manhood.

Hans looked at her, the alcohol giving him a false sense of bravado. "I am going to strongly deal with it. I'm going to finish her."

Sofia's eyes widened, a flicker of excitement crossing her petite face. "You mean you're going to kill her?" she asked, her lustful voice hushed but eager.

Hans nodded, his vision swimming. "Yes. I can't see any other way out."

Nadia leaned in closer, her confident and hot breath against his ear. "You have to be brave, Hans. Do what you need to do. Take control of your life."

Sofia nodded in agreement. "You're strong. Don't let her ruin you. You deserve to be happy."

Their words, though twisted and dark, filled Hans with a sense of validation. For the first time, he felt like these two street prostitutes actually understood his predicament, even if their support was rooted in their own perverse excitement. The alcohol and their encouragement combined to create a dangerous cocktail of false confidence and resolve for Hans.

The conversation took a more intimate turn as the night progressed. Nadia and Sofia led Hans out of the bar, guiding him to a nearby seedy hotel. The neon lights of the city flickered overhead as they made their way through the streets, Hans barely aware of his surroundings. The promise of another physical release, combined with their dark encouragement, seemed like a refuge from his painful life.

As they reached the hotel room, the two girls deftly emptied Hans's wallet and took out the remaining money, their cunning smiles betraying their true intentions. Hans, too intoxicated to notice, fell deeper into their web, unaware of the calculated precision with which they relieved him of his cash.

In the privacy of the hotel room, the night descended into a blur of hedonistic abandon. Hans lost himself in the sensation of their lusty bodies, the warmth of their skin against his, the taste of their kisses mingling with the bitter tang of whiskey. Nadia and Sofia moved with practised ease, their touches both demanding and soothing their customer, their tongues mingled with Hans to create a fervour of high sexual excitement.

Their intimacy was unusually raw and intense, a stark contrast to the cold and brutal encounters he had endured with Anna. For this night, Hans felt powerful and in control. Their words of encouragement fuelled his delusion of strength and dominance. The women kissed his manhood, caressed his chest and voiced a chorus of seductive approval, urging him to take what he wanted with aggression and lust.

In the dimly lit seedy hotel room, the two women expertly began to please Hans, their practised movements revealing the depth of their expertise in their trade.

Sophia, with her delicate touch, and Nadia, with her bold approach, worked in tandem, with their actions choreographed to perfection. Hans, desperate for female touch and deeply intoxicated, found himself lost in the overwhelming pleasure they provided.

Clothes were discarded very early at the onset, leaving Hans and the two women entangled into a complete state of nakedness. The women took turns indulging him, each one expertly pleasing his manhood with her wet mouth, bringing him closer to his climax. They stop licking just when he was about to come, taking him to another higher level of pleasure and sexual madness. Hans became a slave to their sex games, playing with abandon and allowing the two girls to take him to pleasure heaven and back repeatedly.

Sophia then took Hans' manhood into her own control, and started licking it like a candy to further fuel his passion. Nadia watched her act with lustful eyes and started using her practised techniques to keep Hans on the edge, drawing loud moans, vulgar obscenities and pleas from his lips. The women laughed seductively and encouraged Hans to become more and more vulgar, bold and cheap with his choice of words, while they worked their magic on him.

The night became a relentless cycle of pleasure and debauchery, each moment more intense than the last. Hans kept thrusting deep into their bodies through the night, emptying his frustrations, loneliness and sexual hunger into their willing and wet orifices. He held the women tightly with their hair and banged his frustrations into their willing slavish bodies, while uttering unheard of obscenities.

The women's vast sexual experience was evident in their every caress and every move. They took turns showing Hans the tricks of their trade, each trick designed to heighten his senses and drive him deeper into a deeper state of ecstasy.

Sophia's subtle, teasing touches contrasted with Nadia's more assertive advances, creating a dynamic interplay that kept Hans on the edge of his desire. The room echoed with loud vulgar cries and the rustle of the sheets, the atmosphere thick with a blend of Hans' sexual hunger and ladies' practised seduction.

As the night progressed, the two women transitioned from one sexual technique to another. Hans' needs were met with slavish willingness. They anticipated his reactions, rapidly adjusting their twin naked bodies to satisfy his pervert demands.

For Hans, it was a night of unparalleled sexual indulgence, a temporary escape from his troubled reality. The girl's expertise and his own sexual lust combined to create a night that was both intoxicating and unforgettable, a testament to the complex interplay of human desire and professional skill.

As dawn began to break, the reality of his situation began to creep back in. The haze of alcohol and lust started to fade, leaving behind a gnawing emptiness. Hans found himself lying between the naked frames of Nadia and Sofia, their breaths soft and even. His mind raced with the enormity of what he had confessed to them, with the weight of his intentions settling heavily on his chest.

In the quiet moments of the early morning, Hans felt a flicker of self-doubt. The path he was considering was dark and irreversible, and the thought of actually carrying out Anna's execution filled him with a cold dread. But the hazy voices of Nadia and Sofia echoed in his mind, their encouragement mingling with his own frustration.

Hans slipped out of the bed, careful not to wake the sleeping woman. He stood by the window, looking out at the Zurich city as it stirred to life. The paper with the names and numbers was still burning holes in his pocket, a grim reminder of the choices he had to make.

Hans knew he was teetering on the edge of an abyss, and the night's escapades had only pushed him closer to the brink. The validation he had sought in the arms of strange women had given him a false sense of courage, but now, in the light of the morning, he felt more lost than ever.

Returning to the streets and slowly walking home, Hans stared at the road ahead as the weight of his actions pressed down on him. He had reached a point of no return, and the path ahead was shrouded in darkness. The night with Nadia and Sofia had been a temporary escape, but the reality of his grim situation remained unchanged.

Hans closed his eyes momentarily, with the faces of Anna and Lukas haunting his thoughts. The desire for revenge and the need for resolution warred within him, leaving him suspended in a state of turmoil. The choice he faced was one that would define the rest of his life, and the gravity of it threatened to consume him.

As he kept walking, the voices of Nadia and Sofia still echoed in his mind, urging him to be brave, to take control. But Hans knew that the true battle was within himself, and the outcome was far from certain.

The darkness was looming close, and he was left to grapple with the inner demons that threatened to drag him to hell.

CHAPTER 10

The Divorce Discussion

The air in the Keller household was heavy with unspoken tension, and an awkward silence that seemed to permeate every corner of the home. The strained relationship between Hans and Anna had reached its breaking point, and Anna knew that she could no longer delay the inevitable divorce conversation. She had to confront Hans about the possibility of divorce and find a way to free herself from the suffocating grip of their marriage.

One evening, after a particularly brutal and meaningless argument over dinner, Anna decided that it was time. She couldn't continue living in this state of constant turmoil. Taking a deep breath, she walked into the living room where Hans was sitting, sipping his glass of whiskey. The fading light from the fireplace was casting long shadows on his face, the emotions of anger and frustration very evident on his face.

"Hans, we need to talk," Anna said, her voice steady but mixed with a hint of impatience.

Hans was acutely aware of Anna's intentions to seek a divorce; the subtle hints and the cold distance between them gave him enough clues. Yet, he maintained a facade of obliviousness, interacting with her as if their marriage was still intact. He wanted to listen from her mouth.

Every morning, he greeted her with a forced smile, engaging in mundane conversations while suppressing the turmoil within. His act was a desperate attempt to hold onto the semblance of normalcy. He observed her divorce preparations in silence, his mind plotting darkly while he pretended not to notice the growing chasm between them.

Hans feigned utmost ignorance. He looked up, his eyes narrowing. "What is it now, Anna?" he replied, his tone cold and impatient as well.

Anna took a seat across from him, the coffee table a symbolic barrier between them. She clasped her hands together, gathering her thoughts before speaking. "I've been thinking a lot about us, about our marriage, and I have come to a decision."

Hans leaned back in his chair, swirling the golden liquid in his glass. "Ah? And what decision is that?"

Anna took another deep breath, her heart pounding in her chest. "I think we should get a divorce!"

Hans's hand froze expertly, the glass hovering mid-air. For a moment, he said nothing, his eyes locked onto Anna's with an intensity that made her shiver.

Then he placed the whiskey glass down with a deliberate slowness, his expression hardening. "You think we should get a divorce," he repeated, his voice flat and devoid of emotion.

"Yes," Anna replied, her voice firm. "I can't continue living like this, Hans. We are both miserable, and it's not fair to either of us. We need to move on with our lives."

Hans's eyes flashed with anger. "Move on with our lives? Is that what you think? That you can just walk away and start afresh with a younger man?"

Anna's resolve wavered, but she held her ground. "Yes, Hans. I believe it's the best thing for both of us. We've tried to make this work, but it's clear that we cannot make this work."

Hans stood up abruptly, his chair scraping against the wooden floor. He began to pace the room, his hands clenched into fists. "You're not leaving me, Anna. I won't let you leave me like this."

Anna watched him, a mix of fear and sadness in her eyes. "Hans, please. This is not about you. It is about what is best for us. We are toxic together. You know that."

Hans stopped pacing and turned to face her, his expression one of desperation and anger. "And what about Lukas? Is this about him? You think you can just run off with him and live happily ever after?"

Anna shook her head, her eyes filling with sadness. "This is not about Lukas either. It is about what is best for us. We have grown apart, Hans. We've hurt each other so much that there's nothing left. I need to find my own happiness, and so do you."

Hans's face contorted with rage. "Happiness? You think you'll find happiness without me? We've been through too much together for you to just throw it all away."

Anna stood up, her hands trembling. "Hans, listen to yourself. This isn't love. This is possession. You can't control me. You can't keep me trapped in a marriage that's destroying us both."

Hans took a step towards her, his voice rising. "I won't let you leave, Anna. Do you hear me? I won't let you leave."

Anna's heart raced, but she refused to back down. "You don't have a choice, Hans. I've already spoken to a lawyer. I have started the divorce process."

Hans's eyes widened in mock shock. "A lawyer? You've already—" His voice broke off with a practiced pause. He turned away, running a hand through his hair. "How could you do this without talking to me first?"

Anna's voice was soft but resolute. "Because I knew you would react like this. I had to make sure I had a way out. Hans, please understand. This is not easy for me either."

Hans turned back to face her, his eyes filled with a mix of betrayal and hurt. "I thought we could fix this, Anna. I thought we could find a way."

Anna shook her head, tears spilling down her cheeks. "We've tried, Hans. We've tried so many times. But every time, we end up hurting each other more. I can't do this anymore."

Hans watched her, the reality of her words sinking in. He felt a crushing sense of defeat, his world crumbling around him. "And what about everything we've built? Our home, our life?"

Anna wiped her tears, her voice trembling. "We'll figure it out. We can be civil, divide things fairly. But we can't keep pretending that this marriage is salvageable."

Hans stood up again, thinking hard and fast, with his movements slow and deliberate. This is not about things, he thought to himself.

He walked to the window, staring out at the city lights. "I never thought it would come to this," he said quietly. "I always believed we could make it work."

Anna joined him at the window, their reflections shining in the glass. "So did I, Hans. But sometimes, love isn't enough. We've lost ourselves in this marriage. It's time to find ourselves again."

For a moment, they stood there, the remnants of their love framing a fragile connection between them. But the moment passed, and Hans pulled away, the toxic reality of their current situation settling heavily on his shoulders.

"I'll talk to the lawyer as well," he said, his voice barely above a whisper. "We will do this the right way."

Anna nodded, her heart breaking for the man she had once loved so deeply. "Thank you, Hans, for your understanding."

Hans looked at her one last time, the weight of their shared history hanging between them. "Goodbye, Anna," he said, his voice filled with a finality that left no room for doubt.

"Goodbye, Hans," she replied, her voice steady despite the tears in her eyes.

As Hans watched her walk away, he felt a hollow emptiness settle in his chest. He had lost her, and with her, a part of himself. The road ahead was uncertain, but he knew that he had to face it alone. The darkness that had consumed their marriage was behind them now, and it was time to step into the light, no matter how painful the journey might be.

As Hans stood alone in the dimly lit living room, his mind began to race with dark calculations. He knew that the divorce process, even with mutual consent, could take anywhere from one to two months to finalise.

This narrow window of time filled him with a sense of urgency and dread. Hans's thoughts twisted towards a sinister solution. He had to eliminate Anna before she could escape the binds of their marriage and move into the arms of Lukas.

The clock was ticking, and with each passing day, the pressure mounted. The need to act decisively, to reclaim control in the most final way grew more urgent. The timelines pushed him closer to the edge of an irreversible decision.

He opened his drawer and retrieved the crumpled piece of paper with the list of mafia contacts he had received from Karl. A devilish smile crept across his face as he thought about Anna's foolish plans for her future.

The paper in his hand would ensure that all her plans would be buried forever.

CHAPTER 11

The Albanian Gang

Hans's resolve had crystallised into a cold, hard determination. The conversation with Anna had left him with a stark realisation that he had a limited window of time to act. The thought of Anna slipping away from him, and finding happiness with Lukas, was unbearable. Driven by a twisted sense of ownership and vengeance, he decided to pursue the darkest option available to him.

Hans stepped out of his home and made his way to the nearby tram stop, the familiar sound of Zurich's public transport system providing a momentary distraction from his grim thoughts. He boarded Tram 4, his mind racing as he took a seat by the window, watching the city blur past.

The clean, orderly streets of Zurich seemed worlds apart from the seedy underworld he was about to enter. He glanced around at the other passengers, feeling a strange detachment from the normalcy of their daily routines.

After a few stops, Hans transferred to Bus 32, which would take him deeper into downtown Zurich. The bus ride felt endless, each stop bringing him closer to the run-down building where he was to meet the goons.

The city's polished exterior began to give way to darker streets and dilapidated buildings. Hans got off at his stop and walked the remaining distance, his footsteps echoing on the cracked pavement.

He approached the decayed building, its windows barely hanging and graffiti covering the walls, a stark contrast to the pristine Zurich city he was used to living in. With a deep breath, Hans prepared himself and entered the building, ready to confront the evil within.

Hans approached the door, his heart pounding with a mix of fear and anticipation. He knocked twice, as instructed, and waited. The door creaked open, revealing a tall, broad-shouldered Albanian man with a scar running down the side of his face.

"You Hans?" the man asked, his heavily accented voice was low and rough.

Hans nodded, his throat dry. "Yes. Karl has sent me."

The man stepped aside, allowing Hans to enter. The interior of the building was dimly lit, the air thick with the smell of cigarette smoke and dampness. The man led Hans down a narrow hallway to a small, sparsely furnished room. A single bare bulb hung from the ceiling, casting a harsh light over a table and two chairs.

Sitting at the table was another Albanian man in his forties with a scarred face, his hair greying at the temples and his eyes cold and calculating.

"Sit," the man said with a heavy accent, motioning to the chair opposite him.

Hans sat down, his hands trembling slightly. The man across from him leaned back in his chair, studying Hans with a piercing gaze.

"I understand you are looking for a solution to a problem," the man began, his voice deep and measured.

Hans nodded, swallowing hard. "Yes. I need someone eliminated."

The man raised an eyebrow. "Eliminated? You mean killed."

Hans felt a shiver run down his spine at the man's bluntness, but he nodded again. "Yes. Killed."

The man leaned forward, steepling his fingers. "Tell me about the target."

Hans took a deep breath, his voice trembling slightly as he spoke. "Her name is Anna. She's my wife. We are in the process of getting a divorce, but... I can't let her go. She's planning to leave me for another man." Hans, heart pounding, conveyed his sinister request to the Albanian goon, his voice unable to hide his desperation.

The goon, an imposing figure with a scarred face, leaned back and let out a hearty laugh. "You want your wife murdered? We are getting a lot of these requests nowadays!," he said, his eyes gleaming with amusement.

The casualness of his response sent a shiver down Hans's spine, the stark reality of his decision settling in. The goon's confidence was unnerving, making the grim task ahead seem both terrifyingly real and disturbingly simple.

When Hans finished, the man nodded slowly. "I see. And how do you want this done?"

Hans hesitated, the weight of his decision pressing down on him. "I... I don't know. I just want it to be quick and clean."

The man smiled cunningly, shaking his head. "Quick and clean is one option, but there are other ways. More painful, and more elaborate. It depends on the message you want to send."

Hans felt a pang of horror at the man's words, but he also felt a dark curiosity. "What are the options?" he asked, his voice barely above a whisper.

The man leaned back in his chair, his eyes gleaming with a cold light, and let out a chuckle.

"Depends on how much you hate your wife! There are many ways to eliminate someone. Poison, for instance, can be quick or slow, depending on the type."

"A car accident can be staged to look like an unfortunate mishap. Then there's the more personal approach—stabbing, staged suicide or even strangulation. These methods are more intimate, more painful. Depends on what you like!" goon stared at Hans keenly while he explained his tricks of the trade!

Hans felt his stomach churn, but he forced himself to listen. "And... the more painful methods. What do they involve?"

The man's smile widened. "Stabbing is particularly brutal. Multiple wounds can cause a slow, agonising death. Strangulation is also effective—up close and personal. It's a method that allows you to watch the life drain from their eyes."

Hans felt a cold sweat break out on his forehead. He had never imagined he would be discussing such things, but the anger and hatred within him pushed him forward. "And what about the costs?"

Hans, trying to mask his discomfort, enquired about the cost of the sinister task. The Albanian goon, still amused, leaned in closer and said with a smirk, "The cost? It's always less than the hell she makes you go through every day."

His words were sarcastic and sharp, making Hans cringe as the weight of his decision pressed down on him. The goon's laughter echoed in the dimly lit room, amplifying the gravity of the dark agreement they were about to make.

The man pulled a notepad from his pocket and scribbled a few numbers. He slid it across the table to Hans. "These are the prices for the different methods. The more complex and painful, the higher the cost."

Hans glanced at the numbers, his mind racing. The amounts were staggering, but he had enough saved up to cover even the most expensive option. He looked back at the man, a mix of determination and hate in his eyes. "I want it to be painful. I want her to suffer."

The man nodded, his expression approving. "Good. You need to be certain about this. Once we start, there's no turning back."

Hans felt a surge of resolve. "I am certain."

The man stood up, extending his hand. "Then we have a deal. I'll need a fifty percent down payment upfront, and the rest upon completion."

Hans shook his hand, feeling a sense of finality wash over him. He reached into his pocket and pulled out an envelope filled with cash, handing it to the man. "This is half. You'll get the rest when it's done."

The man took the envelope, nodding. "I'll be in touch with the details. Be ready."

Hans stood up, his legs feeling weak. As he walked out of the building, the reality of what he had just done began to sink in. He had crossed a line, and there was no going back. The darkness within him had taken over, and the path ahead was shrouded in shadows.

He stumbled through the streets, his mind numb. The images of the brutal methods they had discussed played over and over in his head. He was surprised at himself, surprised that he could even consider such barbarity. But the anger and pain had twisted him into someone he no longer recognized.

As he made his way back home, Hans felt a cold, grim satisfaction. Anna would pay for what she had done, for the pain she had caused him. He would make sure of it.

The clock was ticking, and soon, the nightmare would come to an end.

CHAPTER 12

The Dark Desires

The encounter with the Albanian gang had Hans feeling a mixture of fear and excitement. As he walked back to his home, the details of the brutal methods they had discussed swirled in his mind.

The idea of inflicting pain on Anna, of asserting his control in the most final way, ignited something dark and sinister within him. By the time he reached his front door, he was consumed by a twisted sense of anticipation and arousal.

The Keller house was quiet, a stark contrast to the chaos that raged within Hans's mind. He poured himself a glass of whiskey, his hands trembling slightly as he took a long and deep swig. The alcohol enhanced the vivid images playing out in his thoughts—images of Anna in pain, suffering at his command. He felt a shiver run down his spine, a strange mix of lust and arousal going through his veins.

Hans made his way to the bathroom, the tension within him building with each step. He locked the door behind him, the sound of the bolt sliding into place sending a thrill of finality through his thoughts. The small and beautifully tiled bathroom was a sanctuary, a place where he could be alone with his thoughts, free to explore the dark fantasies that had taken hold of him.

He turned on the taps, the hot water filling the bathtub with steam. As he undressed, he caught a glimpse of himself in the mirror. His face seemed tired, his eyes staring back at him with a cold and resentful look. He climbed into the tub, the hot water enveloping him, soothing his tense muscles but doing nothing to quell the fire that burned within his heart.

Hans leaned back, closing his eyes as he let his imagination take over. He pictured Anna, her face contorted in pain, her body suffering with the brutal methods he had discussed with the Albanian mob. He replaced himself with the Albanian goon, visualising himself on the mission to kill Anna.

The idea of stabbing Anna, watching the life drain from her eyes as he plunges the knife into her sensuous body, filled him with a sense of twisted satisfaction. He imagined the sound of her gasps, the feel of her blood on his hands, each detail heightening his own sexual arousal.

He reached down, his hand moving with a deliberate slowness as he stroked his manhood, the rhythm matching the dark fantasies playing out in his mind.

The thought of strangulation came next, the image of his hands around Anna's throat, and squeezing the life out of her. He could almost hear Anna's desperate pleas for mercy. The sound of her begging was sending a shiver of pleasure through his body.

Hans's mind was consumed by dark fantasies of strangling Anna, deriving satisfaction from imagining her terror and helplessness as he asserted his dominance.

Hans's breathing grew heavier and his self-pleasuring strokes became more frantic as the images became more vivid. He imagined the look of shock in Anna's eyes, with the final realisation that Hans had won and she is the ultimate loser. The power, the dominance, the finality of it all was intoxicating. Each fantasy, each brutal scenario, pushed him closer to his own climax.

As he reached the peak of his arousal, Hans's mind fixated on the moment of Anna's death, the life going out of her as she realises that Hans has finally won. He would finally spit on Anna's lifeless and contorted face, now that he has managed to end her story.

Hans stroked his manhood frantically, his breaths coming in short gasps, as he uttered vulgar words out of sheer ecstasy. The sexual release came in a wave of a strong ecstasy, his brain filled with a tornado of raw pleasure and his body shuddering with the intensity of an explosive orgasm. He lay there in the cool water, as he kept ejaculating and emptying himself, his mind awash with the aftermath of his sick pleasure.

The satisfaction, however, was fleeting, and was quickly replaced by a cold emptiness. Hans stared at the ceiling, the reality of his desires settling heavily on him. He had crossed a line within himself, exploring a darkness that he had never known existed. The thrill of power, the arousal that he felt, left him feeling hollower and lonelier than ever before.

As the water grew cold, Hans finally rose from the tub, his body heavy with exhaustion. He wrapped a towel around himself, avoiding his reflection in the mirror. The man he had become, and the depths he had sunk to, were too much to face. He left the bathroom, the steam dissipating behind him, and made his way to the bedroom.

Hans lay down on the bed, the silence of the house pressing in on him. The fantasies that had once seemed so exciting now felt like chains, binding him to a path of darkness and destruction. The arousal, the power, had given way to a crushing sense of despair. He was trapped in his own mind, a prisoner to the desires that had overtaken him.

As he drifted off to sleep, Hans's thoughts returned to the Albanian contract killer and the plan they had set in motion. The clock was ticking, and the time for action was drawing near. The night's dark fantasies would soon become a reality, and there would be no turning back.

In the days that followed his meeting with the Albanian gang, Hans found himself increasingly consumed by thoughts of Anna's impending murder. Each detail he imagined—every grim, brutal scenario—filled him with a thrill and excitement that he hadn't felt in years.

The mundane monotony of his recent life seemed to fade away, replaced by an electric anticipation. The thought of having complete control over Anna's fate, of orchestrating her suffering and demise, was intoxicating. It was a perverse source of power, a dark thrill that sent shivers down his spine.

The fantasies became his constant companion, invading his thoughts at every turn. He savoured the murder's sights and sounds: the look of terror in Anna's eyes, the gasps of pain, the final, desperate struggles. These visions were more exhilarating than anything he had experienced in his recent past, filling the void left by his failing career and broken marriage.

Anna's murder plan gave him a renewed sense of purpose, a dark, twisted goal that eclipsed all else. It was a sinister thrill, a forbidden excitement that both terrified and enthralled him.

Hans knew that he was further down a sinister path from which there would be no return.

CHAPTER 13

The Roleplay

Hans found himself obsessively replaying Anna's murder scenarios in his mind, each iteration more detailed and vivid than the last. These thoughts didn't just occupy his mind—they seeped into his very being, igniting a primal excitement that he hadn't felt in years.

As he went about his daily routine, Hans's mind would drift to the plans he had discussed with the Albanian contract killer. He would imagine the feel of the knife in his own hand, the resistance of flesh and bone as he plunged it into Anna's body.

The thought of her blood, warm and smooth, on his skin sent shivers of pleasure down his spine. The power of holding her life in his hands, of being the orchestrator of her final moments, was an aphrodisiac unlike any other. He felt unusually aroused and horny all the time.

In the solitude of his study, Hans would sip his cheap whisky, close his eyes and let the fantasies take over. He envisioned the struggle, the gasps for breath, the final, desperate look in Anna's eyes. Each imagined detail heightened his arousal, his body responding to the dark, erotic thrill of the power he would wield. He found himself touching his own manhood, his breath quickening as he lost himself in the perverse excitement.

At night, as he lay in bed, the fantasies would return, more vivid and intense. He imagined the moment of confrontation, the rush of adrenaline, the intoxicating mix of fear and power. Hans's body would react, his arousal growing with each dark thought. He would reach down and stroke himself, his hands moving in rhythm with the imagined scenes of brutality and control, his breath ragged with excitement.

The murder plan had become more than just a means to an end; it was a source of profound, sexual pleasure. Hans found himself craving the thrill, the dark excitement that these fantasies brought him. It was a twisted, all-consuming desire that filled the void left by his failing career and broken marriage, giving him a sense of purpose and power that he had long since lost.

One evening, unable to contain his excitement any longer, Hans found himself drawn back to the seedy part of Zurich where he had met Nadia and Sofia. The memories of their last encounter, their encouragement of his dark desires, had lingered in his mind. He remembered the tantalising release they had provided. He needed that sexual release again, and needed to feel the rush of power and control that the orgy with these two women had given him.

As he moved further into the city, the polished facades of the buildings gave way to the seedy lanes of District 5. The atmosphere grew heavier and the streets became darker, as he approached the seedy bar that he knew so well by now. The neon lights flickered ominously, and the hum of low conversations and clinking glasses beckoned him back to the place where he had last found a perverse sense of solace with Nadia and Sophia.

He stumbled into the same bar, the familiar scent of stale beer and smoke enveloping him. His eyes scanned the room, desperately searching for the two women who had become his confidantes in his twisted journey. When he finally spotted them at the end of the bar, his heart raced with anticipation.

Nadia and Sofia greeted him with knowing smiles, their eyes gleaming with a mix of sensuality and excitement. They could see the desperation in his eyes, the barely contained arousal that had driven him back to them.

"Back for more?" Nadia purred, her hand resting on his arm.

Hans nodded, his voice husky with need. "I need to talk. I need... something more."

Sofia leaned in closer, her breath warm against his ear. "Let's go somewhere private," she whispered.

They led him out of the bar and to the same nearby hotel. The neon lights flickered overhead as they made their way through the dimly lit streets. Hans's mind was a whirlwind of dark fantasies and carnal desire, and his body was tense with sexual anticipation.

In the dimly lit hotel room, Hans's gaze lingered hungrily on the two women. Nadia stood tall with her striking red hair cascading down her shoulders. Her sharp green eyes glinted mischievously.

Hans found himself confessing his darkest thoughts once again to them. He described the vivid fantasies that had consumed him, the detailed plans he had imagined for Anna's murder. As he spoke, his excitement grew, and the words were spilling out in an eager rush.

Nadia and Sofia listened with rapt attention, their expressions a mix of fascination and arousal. They encouraged him, and their words were feeding his twisted desires. "You are so strong, Hans," Nadia said, her voice low and sultry. "You have the power to take control of your life. Don't let the bitch win."

Sofia nodded, her hand sliding down his chest. "Do what you need to do, Hans. Take what's yours."

Hans nodded, his voice low and husky. "Yes. And this time, I need something different from you two."

Sofia leaned in closer, her breath warm against his ear. "What do you have in mind?"

Hans took a deep breath, his heart pounding with a mix of anticipation and fear. "I want you to play a role for me. I need you to be Anna."

Nadia raised an eyebrow, intrigued. "Anna? You mean your wife?"

Hans nodded, swallowing hard. "Yes. I need to act out my fantasies, to feel the power and control. I'll pay you more, whatever it takes."

The two women exchanged a glance, their eyes gleaming with interest. "Alright," Sofia said, her voice low and sultry. "We will do it. But you have to be prepared for whatever happens. And it will cost you much more!". The girls laughed together with wild abandon.

Nadia, stepping into the role of Anna, dressed in a sophisticated outfit—a sleek black dress that clung to her curves and a pair of elegant heels. She meticulously applied her makeup, her red lips and dark eyeliner transforming her into the spitting image of Hans's estranged wife, Anna.

Sophia, watching with a mix of anticipation and apprehension, slipped into a classy red outfit herself, though her role was merely to observe. They both inhaled multiple lines of white powder, the potent chemical rush erasing any lingering inhibitions for the night ahead.

As Nadia slipped into character, her demeanour shifted. She was ready to engage in the aggressive sex session that Hans so desperately craved.

"Get down on your knees, Anna, and crawl toward me," Hans hissed under his breath, his voice laced with a commanding edge.

Nadia, playing the role of Anna, crawled towards him with a mock fearful expression.

"Please, Hans," she begged, her voice trembling as she crawled towards Hans on her hands and knees, "Don't hurt me."

Her eager words sent a shiver of animal excitement down his spine, and Hans felt a rush of arousal in his head. He grabbed her hair roughly, his hands shaking with excitement. "You don't get to decide what happens, Anna," he growled, pushing her onto the bed.

Nadia landed on the creaky bed with a soft thud and moaned with wild excitement as she eagerly awaited Hans to join her on the bed.

Sofia, playing the role of a silent observer, watched with wide eyes, her presence heightening the intensity of the encounter. Under the influence of drugs and alcohol, they were much more pliant, more than willing to indulge Hans's every whim.

Under the influence of the white powder, Nadia and Sophia's eyes narrowed to sharp, glassy points, their pupils dilated with a wild intensity. Their breathing became fast and shallow, and each inhale and exhale was a frantic gasp. Their bodies, flushed and feverish, radiated heat, sweat glistening on their skin.

Their movements became more erratic, their laughter more unrestrained, and a dangerous, reckless energy took hold, propelling them into the depths of their dark roleplay with Hans.

They became a willing sex slave to Hans, transposing his anger on Anna on their sensuous, sexual and willing bodies.

Hans's dark anger surged as he climbed the bed and grabbed Nadia by her blonde hair, his grip tightening to inflict maximum pain. His eyes glinted with a twisted pleasure as he yanked her head back, revelling in her gasp of discomfort. The classy black dress she wore became his next target, a symbol of Anna's sophistication that he wanted to desperately destroy.

Slowly, frantically, he began tearing the fabric apart, each rip exposing more of her skin, using his claws and teeth.

His bites on Nadia's body were rough and deliberate, leaving marks on every inch of flesh he uncovered. He took sadistic pleasure in her moans and cries, each pained sound fueling his rage and dark satisfaction with Anna.

The elegant garment, now in tatters, mirrored the chaos within Hans's mind as he continued his brutal assault on the blonde prostitute.

He imagined that it was Anna beneath him, her body writhing in pain and fear. He revelled in the power he felt, the control he had over her. Each slap that landed on Nadia's body, each harsh word spoken to her, was a manifestation of his need to dominate and destroy Anna and her life.

Petite and pretty Sophia watched this with fear and excitement. Her own drug filled mind wanted to be a desperate part of this action. She came to her fours, and crawled towards Hans, begging to be a part of this action.

She unzipped his trousers, took out his manhood and started pleasuring herself with the swelled organ, while Hans continued the assault on the blonde girl.

The threesome encounter grew more intense through the night, bordering on something darker. Fuelled by periodic intake of the white coke lines, the three lost their sense of the right and wrong, and indulged in frantic pursuit of their fantasies and bodily pleasures.

Hans's mind was a storm of violent images, and he found himself lost in the sensation of crushing the two beautiful female bodies, imagining the feel of Anna's skin beneath his hands. The more brutal he became, the more excited he felt, with his sexual arousal reaching new heights.

Nadia and Sofia, under the influence of drugs and alcohol, prodded him on, their words a twisted encouragement. "You're strong, Hans, so strong," Nadia whispered, buried under Hans, her voice now shaky with assault. "Punish me harder, and kill me tonight."

Sofia's wet tongue roamed his body with abandon, her animal touch igniting a fire within Hans. "Tear my body apart," she urged, her eyes gleaming with excitement. "Make Anna pay dearly."

Hans entered Nadia's body with lust, his thrusts into her willing orifice became more frenzied. His grip tightened as he crushed the two widely spread girls beneath him. The room was filled with the sounds of their loud and vulgar moans, the brutal encounter reaching a feverish pitch. He felt a rush of power, a dark thrill that sent shivers down his spine.

As he reached the peak of his arousal, his mind was filled with the image of Anna's terrified face, the sound of her final, desperate breaths. His release came in a wave of dark ecstasy, his body shuddering with the intensity of his ejaculation. He lay on top of the two naked girls, spent and breathless, with his mind reeling from the crazy encounter.

The satisfaction however was fleeting, quickly replaced by the recurring emptiness. Hans stared at the ceiling, the reality of his actions settling heavily on him.

As the drug influence faded, Hans rose from the bed, his body heavy with exhaustion. He looked at Nadia and Sofia, their naked bodies marked by the intensity of the encounter, and felt a pang of guilt.

CHAPTER 14

The Morning After

The encounter in the hotel room had left Hans feeling exhilarated and powerful, but as the adrenaline faded, the brutal reality of what he had done began to sink in. The room was a mess, the air heavy with the scent of sweat and desperation.

Hans turned to look at Nadia and Sofia, their bodies marked by the intensity of his actions. They lay naked on the bed, their breaths shallow and laboured, their eyes closed in exhaustion and drug induced stupor.

Hans felt a wave of shame wash over him as he took in their condition. Nadia's lip was split, and bruises were already forming on her face, breasts, arms and torso. Sofia's face was also swollen, and she had scratches and bite marks covering her entire upper body.

The sight of their battered bodies filled him with a sickening guilt. He had pushed them too far, and let his sick fantasies drive him to a place he did not imagine he could ever go.

He knelt by the bed, his hands trembling as he reached out to touch Nadia's arm. "I'm so sorry," he whispered, his voice choked with emotion. "I didn't mean to hurt you like this."

Nadia opened her eyes slowly, wincing with pain as she moved. "We knew what we were getting into," she replied, her voice weak but steady. "Sometimes, it is more than what we expect," she smiled weakly.

Sofia nodded in agreement, her eyes barely opening under the morning light. "You have a lot of anger, Hans. A lot of darkness. We could see that from the beginning."

Hans swallowed hard, his guilt intensifying. "I don't know what came over me. I just... I couldn't stop."

Nadia reached out and took his hand, her grip surprisingly strong. "You need to find a way to control it, Hans. This path you're on... it's not going to end well for you."

Sofia added, her voice soft, "You have to let go of your anger. Find another way to deal with it."

Hans nodded, tears welling up in his eyes. "I know. I know you're right. But it's so hard. Every time I think about Anna, about what she has done, I just... I can't handle it."

Nadia squeezed his hand gently. "You need to find a way, Hans. For your sake, and for everyone else's. And, come back to us, whenever you need us," she gave him a seductive smile.

Hans sat there for a long time, holding their hands, his mind racing with conflicting emotions. The darkness within him was powerful, but the guilt and shame he felt were just as strong. He had to find a way to reconcile these feelings, to come to terms with his actions and his desires.

Eventually, he helped Nadia and Sofia clean up, offering them as much care as he could. He knew that money couldn't erase the pain he had caused, but he gave them extra wads of cash, hoping it would help in some small way. Girls gleefully collected the extra cash and winked him goodbye.

As he left the hotel room, he couldn't erase the image of their bruised, battered and sensuous bodies from his mind.

The walk home was a blur, and his thoughts were a chaotic mess of guilt, shame, and anger. Hans' clothes were dishevelled and wrinkled, a stark contrast to the pristine streets of Zurich. His shirt was untucked, coat was crumpled and the scent of last night's smells - cigarettes, alcohol and the girl's cheap perfume - clung to him. His once-polished shoes were dirty, and he appeared like a homeless man walking on the streets of Zurich.

As the effects of the previous night's excess with Nadia and Sophia began to wear off, a creeping paranoia took hold of him. Every sound of Zurich streets seemed amplified to him, and every whisper of passerby was a poke at his fragile brain. He pulled his coat tighter around him, as if the woollen barrier could shield him from the prying eyes he imagined all around him. Zurich, the city Hans once loved for its serene beauty, now felt like his prison of judgement and shame.

The rational part of his mind tried to assert itself, reminding him that these were mere strangers, random people he met on roads. But the alcohol and coke withdrawal had left him raw and exposed, with his emotions unbalanced. Every glance felt like a sneer and every smile was a cruel taunt.

He passed a café where a group of young people sat outside, and were sipping their morning coffee. One of them looked up as he walked by, and Hans could swear he saw a smirk. His stomach churned and he even thought to turn and confront him. He couldn't bear the humiliation in that stare of the stranger. He barely managed to keep walking.

He approached a busy intersection, the traffic lights blinking a steady green. A traffic policeman stood nearby, directing the flow of cars with his practised movements. As Hans stepped onto the crosswalk, he could feel the officer's gaze on him. It was as if a spotlight had been turned on Hans, highlighting his every flaw and weakness of his character.

"Keep walking, Hans," he muttered to himself, his heart racing. "It's just in your head."

But he couldn't shake the strange feeling within his head. The policeman's eyes seemed to follow him, boring into his back with unspoken judgement. Hans quickened his pace, nearly stumbling over the footpath as he reached the other side. He risked a glance back and was sure he saw the officer staring at him, as though he knew the dark details of Hans' last night.

Further down the street, Hans passed a row of small shops opening for the day. The scent of fresh bread emerged from a bakery, mingling with the aroma of freshly brewed coffee. Under different circumstances, it might have been comforting. But today, it only made his stomach churn.

As he walked by the bakery, he noticed the shopkeeper, a short, fat man with a happy face, watching him through the window. Their eyes met briefly, and Hans saw the man's expression change from friendly curiosity to wary suspicion. He felt a flush of heat rise to his cheeks and he quickly looked away.

In the next shop, a woman arranging flowers glanced up as he passed. Her smile faltered, replaced by a look of unease. Hans couldn't help but imagine her thoughts.

He tried to convince himself it was all in his head, and was a cruel trick played by his weakened mind. But the withdrawal from coke and the whispers of paranoia were relentless. Each shopkeeper's careful glance, and each customer's look, seemed to confirm his fears. He was a marked man, with his sins written on his face for all of Zurich to see.

The final blow came as he neared a small park where children played under the watchful eyes of their parents. Hans usually found a lot of solace in the innocent laughter of children. But today, even this sanctuary was failing him.

A group of children playing stopped and stared at him as he walked by. One of the younger ones, a little girl with cute ponytails, hid behind her mother's leg, her wide eyes filled with fear. Hans' heart sank. Did he really appear so monstrous and so tainted, that even a child could sense it?

The mother cast him a wary glance, and pulled her daughter closer. Hans quickened his pace, wanting nothing more than to escape the suffocating judgement that seemed to follow him wherever he went. He could feel their eyes on his back, as his shame overtook his sanity.

He turned down a quieter street, with his breathing coming in gasps. He needed to get home fast, to the safety of his apartment, where he could hide from the staring eyes and their judgments. His mind raced, replaying the perverse events of the night before, and each pleasurable memory was now a sharp regret.

Hans boarded the Zurich tram with a heavy heart, the previous night's events weighing on him heavily.

As the tram glided through the city, every glance from fellow passengers felt piercing and judgmental. The bustling streets outside seemed to mock him, as if each passerby was a silent witness to his shameful deeds.

He imagined as if he could almost hear other passengers' whispers, imagining their scornful laughter as if they all knew the depths of his depravity.

The short tram journey felt very long, his mind racing with paranoid thoughts. Each stop brought in more people, their casual conversations and laughter amplifying his sense of exposure.

Hans shrank into his seat, his skin prickling with embarrassment, convinced that his darkest secrets were laid bare for all to see. The city he once navigated with confidence now felt like an open court, with every street and corner echoing his guilt and disgrace.

The terrible side effects of the coke wearing off was making him paranoid and fearful. All of his brash confidence wore off, and he became a worse version of himself. By the time he reached his stop, Hans was a nervous wreck.

CHAPTER 15

Witnessing the Tornado

As he neared his home, Hans noticed that the lights were on in his house. His heart skipped a beat, a mixture of fear and curiosity compelling him to approach the home quietly. He hadn't expected Anna to be home, and certainly not with any company. His footsteps faltered as he saw two silhouettes moving inside, with their shapes illuminated by the warm glow of the lamps.

Hans walked closer, the high shrubs and the nearby trees concealing him. He positioned himself near the tall French windows that faced the living room. As the curtains were open, it offered him a clear view of the scene unfolding inside. What he saw inside, froze his mind.

Anna was there, her laughter echoing softly as she moved with grace and ease. Lukas was with her, his hands on her waist as they danced to the soft music playing from the stereo.

Hans watched, his heart pounding with a mix of rage and humiliation. They were celebrating, their joy a stark contrast to the turmoil and filth that consumed him all night.

As he stood there, hidden in the shadows, Hans felt a sickening twist of anger mixed with arousal. He couldn't tear his eyes away from the scene inside.

Anna and Lukas moved together with a familiarity and ease that spoke of their deep connection. Hans watched as they danced and shared a tender kiss. The passion between them was so evident, that it was painful for Hans to witness.

Anna's slender fingers trailed down Lukas's chest, her touch meant to tease him. Lukas responded by pulling her body closer. Their bodies pressed together as they kissed each other more deeply.

Hans felt a surge of jealousy and desire, his fists clenching at his sides as he watched their intimacy. The sight of their warm bodies moving together in a dance of love and lust was both arousing and enraging to his fragile mind.

Unable to look away, Hans's breath quickened as he watched Anna unbutton Lukas's shirt, with her movements slow and deliberate. Lukas's hands caressed her back, and his touch filled with a tenderness that Hans had long forgotten. The way they looked at each other, with deep love and desire, was a knife to Hans's heart.

Hans felt a flush of heat rising through his body. His anger was mingling with a dark, voyeuristic excitement. He always perversely fantasised Anna with someone else, however when it was happening now, he was confused, aroused and enraged.

Hans leaned closer to the window, his breath fogging the window glass as he watched Anna slide Lukas's shirt off his shoulders. Anna's hands traced the contours of Lukas' broad chest, her fingers lingering on the lines of his tough muscles.

Lukas's hands moved to the sides of Anna's dress, and he lifted her dress slowly as their kisses grew more passionate. Hans's heart raced as he watched the dress fall away, revealing Anna's sensual body to Lukas's hungry stare.

She stood naked and confident before Lukas, her beautiful skin glowing in the soft light, her sensuous curves accentuated by the shadows.

Hans's breath was caught in his throat as Lukas kissed his way down Anna's neck, making her moan with pleasure. His hands were caressing her breasts with a tenderness that made Hans's chest tighten with envy.

The sight of them together, so intimately connected, filled him with a burning rage and an overwhelming arousal. He felt a perverse rush of blood to his manhood, his body reacting to the erotic scene before him despite the anger that overtook his brain.

Hans's hand moved to the front of his pants. His fingers were trembling as he opened the front of his trouser, freed his manhood and started rubbing himself. Conflicting emotions of shame and fury overtook Hans, heightening his own arousal as he watched Lukas guide Anna to the couch.

They lay down together, their naked bodies entwined, their movements fluid and bodies synchronised in a lover's dance. Hans's eyes were locked on them as they made tender love, their passion raw and unfiltered. Anna's moans of raw pleasure filled the room, her head thrown back in ecstasy as Lukas entered her and thrust deep within her.

The sight was both torturous and intoxicating, each sound and movement further fueling the flames of Hans's jealousy and perverse excitement. As Hans watched them, his own humiliating arousal grew. He stroked his manhood with increasing urgency, with his eyes never leaving the lovemaking scene inside.

Anna's intimate cries grew louder, with her body arching forward in response to Lukas's deep thrusts inside her. Hans felt a surge of shame and anger at the sight, his own desire filling his brain and overtaking all of his thoughts.

The intensity of his feelings reached a peak as he watched Anna reach her loud climax, with her body trembling with the force of her orgasm. Lukas followed soon after, his face contorted with pleasure as he emptied himself deep within her.

The sight was too much for Hans, and he felt his own ejaculation exploding, with a mix of weakness, shame and arousal that left him breathless and shaking desperately.

Hans leaned against the wall, his breathing in gasps as he tried to regain control over his body. His limp, spent manhood was now a sign of weakness that had overtaken his mind and soul. He pushed his organ inside his pants as he struggled to clean his slippery palms with the side of his pants. His unwashed body reeked of peculiar smells now, as he struggled to reclaim any resemblance of normalcy.

He knew they had crossed a line. The desire to destroy Anna, and to reclaim the power Hans felt that he had lost, was stronger than ever within him.

But as he stood there, watching them through the window, he also felt a growing sense of despair. He felt weak, damaged and directionless. The path he was on was a dark and dangerous one, and he was unsure if he could ever find his way back.

Hans turned his eyes away from the window, as his mind reeled in a chaotic storm of emotions. This complicated night was the lowest ebb of his life. He never felt so spent, so weak and so powerless ever in his life before.

As he looked away from the window, he knew that the days ahead would be filled with even more turmoil and darkness.

The darkness of his perverse fantasies had unfortunately become too much of a reality for him, and he did not know the way out.

CHAPTER 16

The Confrontation

Hans stood outside his home, the weight of the recent events pressing heavily on his shoulders. The raw, visceral pleasure he had felt moments before had dissipated, leaving behind a bitter taste of humiliation and defeat.

As he stared at the tall French windows of his home, he could still see the faint silhouettes of Anna and Lukas in each other's comforting arms.

It should have been me, thought Hans bitterly. The sight of two naked bodies stirred a mix of rage and determination within him. It was time to face the man who had taken his place in Anna's life.

With a deep breath, Hans squared his shoulders, straightened his frame and walked to the front door. His hand trembled slightly as he turned the key in the lock, the familiar click echoing through the quiet night.

The door creaked open, and Hans stepped inside, the warmth of his house enveloping him. He could hear soft murmurs and the rustle of sheets from the living room, the intimate sounds of a couple settling down after a passionate encounter.

Hans walked down the hallway, his footsteps muffled by the plush carpet. As he approached the living room, the murmurs grew louder, the voices more distinct. He could feel his heart pounding inside his rib cage.

Hans was secretly worried that anything could happen now. Lukas can maybe get aggressive and maybe even kill him, while he was still planning Anna's murder.

He waited around the corner and stopped, his presence immediately felt by the two people on the couch. Anna and Lukas looked up, their eyes widening in surprise and shock.

"Hans?" Anna quickly pulled a blanket around her naked body, her cheeks flushing with embarrassment.

Lukas, on the other hand, remained seated, his expression unreadable. He met Hans's gaze with a steady calmness, with a hint of defiance in his eyes.

"You're back early," Lukas said, his voice low and measured.

Hans took a step forward, his red eyes locked onto Lukas's. "I see you've made yourself comfortable in my house," he replied.

Lukas stood up slowly, his movements deliberate and unhurried. He was naked, and he very slowly pulled his jeans up.

"We need to talk, Hans," Lukas said, his tone firm but not hostile.

Hans felt a surge of rage. "Talk? About what, Lukas? About how you've been screwing my wife in my own house?"

Lukas didn't flinch, and he replied back with a steady gaze. "About what's really happening here. About why Anna felt she had to find comfort with someone else."

Anna stepped forward, her voice trembling. "Please, let's not do this. Not like this, plea—"

Hans turned to her, his eyes filled with a mix of hurt and anger. "Not like this? How else should we do it, Anna? How should I react to finding another man in my home, in my own bed?"

Lukas put a hand on Anna's shoulder, gently guiding her to sit back down. "Hans, we all need to be honest with each other. This situation is more complicated than just infidelity."

Hans's fists clenched at his sides, his nails digging into his palms. "Complicated? It's pretty damn simple from where I'm standing."

Lukas remained calm, his voice steady. "Hans, Anna has been unhappy for a long time. This is not happening lightly. We have been friends for months, and I've seen how much she struggled in this marriage with you."

Hans's eyes flashed with fury. "And you thought you could just step in and take my place?"

Lukas shook his head. "No, Hans. I did not want to take your place. But Anna needed someone, and you were never there for her."

Anna's eyes filled with tears. "Hans, I tried to tell you. I tried to make you see how unhappy I was, but you never listened."

Hans felt a pang of guilt mingled with his anger. He had seen the signs, the distance growing between them, but he had been too wrapped up in his own misery to truly address it.

"So, this is my fault, then? Because I wasn't the perfect husband? He retorted.

Lukas took a step closer, his eyes almost earnest.

"It's not about fault, Hans. It's about recognizing that things are not working in your marriage with Anna and trying to find a way to move forward."

Hans glared at him, his fists still clenched. "And you think sleeping with my wife is the way to move forward?"

Anna stood up, wiping her tears. "Hans, please. This isn't just about the physical act of sex. It is about the connection I've lost with you. The intimacy and the love, It has been gone for so long."

Hans's anger flared again. "And you think you found that with him?" He poked his finger at Lukas' chest, his hand shaking with rage.

Lukas met Hans's gaze, unflinching. "I care about Anna, Hans. I never meant for this to happen, but it did. And now we need to deal with it."

Hans took a deep breath, trying to control the whirlwind of emotions inside him. He wanted to smash his Lukas's face, shatter his ribs, and erase that confident smile from Lukas' face.

In his mind, Hans imagined wild scenes of revenge. He imagined himself like a stranger sneaking through the night to catch Lukas off guard. The satisfaction of a tightly clenched fist meeting Lukas's smug face played out again and again in Hans' mind. Each tight blow was a satisfying release of his pent-up anger on Lukas.

He imagined himself dragging Lukas to a secluded spot and to wrap his body with brutal punches and kicks. With every punch and kick, Hans visualised Lukas's confident smirk turning to a grimace of pain. He wanted to overcome the younger man's strength with his sudden attack, and to watch as the arrogance gets drained from Lukas's eyes, replaced by fear and pain.

In this imaginary confrontation, Hans felt a surge of energy coursing through his veins, transforming his weak, alcohol dependent frame into a body full of unexpected power.

He imagined Lukas charging at him, his muscles rippling with youthful arrogance. But Hans fantasised himself with the agility of a seasoned fighter. Hans sidesteps the assault, using Lukas's momentum against him. With a calculated move, he struck Lukas in the side, a precise blow that sent the younger man staggering. Hans's drug fuelled mind imagined each motion with meticulous detail, a choreography of dominance where he defeated Lukas at every turn.

He day-dreamed about grabbing Lukas by his collar. Hans' grip unyielding as he pulled Lukas close to him, with their faces mere inches apart. He whispered words of fury and betrayal, each word a dagger aimed at Lukas's confidence. He could see the flicker of doubt in Lukas's eyes, and feel the tremor in his once-steady hands.

With a final, decisive push, Hans fantasised hurling Lukas to the ground, standing over him as the victor. In this moment, Hans was no longer the broken, defeated man; he was a force of nature, reclaiming his dignity and power with every breath.

In his drug fueled imagination, Hans had enacted a strong revenge against Lukas. He envisioned Lukas dropping to his knees, and pleading with Hans for mercy. The violent fantasy, vivid and intoxicating, offered Hans a temporary balm to his wounded male pride, a fleeting illusion of regaining control over his spiralling life.

But as the vivid daydreams faded, reality crashed back in, highlighting the futility of his thoughts. Hans knew that these imaginations, born from his addictions, could never truly compensate for the fragility he felt in his current state.

He looked at the confident young Lukas, looking strong and unbeatable, having had an intimate intercourse with his beautiful wife. Hans felt defeated.

"So, what now? You think we can just sit down and talk this out? Hans retorted.

Lukas nodded. "We have to. For Anna's sake, and for your own."

Hans's mind raced. The idea of sitting down and calmly discussing the situation seemed impossible. The image of Anna and Lukas naked together, the intimacy they shared, was too fresh and too painful. Yet, a part of him knew that a discussion was inevitable, and perhaps necessary.

Anna reached out, taking Hans's hand. "Please, Hans. Let's talk. We owe it to ourselves to try and find a way through this."

She had now covered her naked pretty frame with an elegant and expensive wrap-around, which was making her allure even more irresistible to Hans. Anna smelled heavenly, covered with an seemingly expensive perfume, a far cry from the cheap perfumes of Nadia and Sophia, which he had sniffed all night.

Hans looked at her, seeing the pain and desperation in her eyes. The anger inside him began to wane, replaced by a deep, aching sadness. "Alright," he said quietly. "We will talk. But this isn't going to be easy."

They all sat down around the table, with the tension in the room palpable. Hans looked at Lukas, his eyes narrowing. "How long has this been going on?"

Lukas sighed, running a hand confidently through his hair. "A few weeks. It started as just friendship, but it grew into something more, very quickly."

Hans's jaw tightened. "And you didn't think to stop? To consider the consequences of sleeping with a married woman?"

Lukas met his gaze. "I tried, Hans, to be honest. But the feelings were mutual. And we couldn't ignore them."

Anna's voice was gentle. "Hans, I never meant to hurt you. But I was so lonely, so lost. I didn't realise when I got lost in Lukas' love and tenderness."

Hans's heart ached at her words. He had felt the same loneliness, and the exact same sense of loss. But he had turned to darker avenues to cope with his pain, which now seemed even more twisted in the harsh light of this confrontation.

"So, what do we do now?" Hans asked, his voice heavy with resignation.

Lukas spoke carefully. "We need to be honest with each other. About our feelings, and about our future. This situation is not sustainable. We need to figure out what happens next."

Hans nodded slowly. "I don't know if I can forgive this. But I also know that things can't go back to the way they were."

Anna squeezed his hand. "Hans, I'm so sorry. I never wanted this. But I need to be true to myself, and so do you."

Hans looked at her, seeing the truth in her eyes. The love they once shared had been eroded by years of neglect and pain.

Hans gathered himself, looked at Anna and Lukas and said, "I don't know what the future holds. But I know that I can't keep living like this. I need to find a way forward, whatever that means."

Hans knew that the path ahead would be dangerous and uncertain, but it was a path he was ready to face.

CHAPTER 17

Understanding Lukas

The night had been long and arduous, but finally, it came to an end. As the first light of dawn began to creep into the room, Hans felt a strange mix of exhaustion and strange relief.

He watched as Lukas prepared to leave, the tension between them still palpable. Anna had gone to the kitchen to fetch some water, leaving the two men alone for a moment.

Lukas gathered his things, pausing at the door. He turned to Hans, a smug smile playing at the corners of his lips. His tone was low, just above a whisper, ensuring Anna couldn't hear.

"You know, Hans," Lukas began, his voice dripping with contempt, "Anna is really irresistible in bed! The way her body responds to my touches, and the way she touches me down is heavenly. Above all, listening to her moan and grunt under my assault, it is all so very satisfying! You are surely going to miss her in bed, buddy."

Hans felt a surge of rage flare up within him, but he fought to keep his expression neutral.

"Is that supposed to make me feel better, Lukas?" he replied, his voice tight.

Lukas chuckled softly, shaking his head. "No, Hans, it's not. It's just a little reality check. She's moved on, and maybe you should too. You couldn't keep her satisfied in bed, but I can."

Hans clenched his fists at his sides, his knuckles turning white. "You think this is a game, Lukas? You think you've won something?"

Lukas's smile widened. "It's not about winning, Hans. It's about being there for her, giving her the physical pleasure that she needs. And right now, you clearly can't do it."

Hans took a step closer, his voice a low growl. "Watch yourself, Lukas. You have no idea what you're getting into."

Lukas raised an eyebrow, straightened his shoulder and seemed unfazed. "I think I know exactly what I'm getting into. And trust me, Hans, she is worth every moment," he replied with an evil smirk.

Just then, Hans understood Lukas and what he stood for. Hans watched Lukas's demeanour shift, and a chilling realisation began to form in his mind. Lukas, a struggling artist, had found a golden opportunity in Anna, a successful art business woman.

It became clear that Lukas was not only interested in her for romance but was also leveraging her status to maximise his own profit potential.

The reality dawned on Hans with brutal clarity. Lukas's smooth talk and affectionate gestures were all part of a calculated strategy to secure his own future at Anna's expense.

Hans's jealousy turned into a bitter realisation of how he had been outmanoeuvred by a young boy. He saw through Lukas's facade, recognizing the opportunistic nature that lurked beneath his polished outer surface.

The realisation fueled his anger and desperation, intensifying his determination to regain control of his life and dismantle the web of deceit Lukas had spun around Anna.

Anna returned just in time, holding a glass of water. She looked between the two men, sensing the tension but unaware of the words exchanged. Lukas turned to her, his expression softening instantly. He took the glass from her hand, setting it aside before pulling her into a slow, sensual kiss.

Hans stood there, watching as Lukas's hands caressed Anna's back, pulling her closer. Anna responded with equal passion, her fingers tangling in Lukas's hair as they deepened the kiss.

Lukas threw a glance at Hans, as he caressed Anna's soft posterior and winked an eye at Hans.

The sight was a knife to Hans's heart, a visual reminder of everything he had lost.

Their kiss seemed to last forever, their bodies pressed tightly together, oblivious to Hans's presence. He could see the intimacy, the connection they shared, and it filled him with a bitter mix of rage and envy. His breath quickened, his fists clenching and unclenching as he struggled with his conflicting emotions.

When they finally broke apart, Lukas looked over Anna's shoulder, meeting Hans's gaze with a triumphant glint in his eye. "Take care, Hans. Try to move on. It will be better for you."

With that, Lukas turned and walked out the door with a winner's stride, leaving Hans standing there, seething with a mixture of humiliation and rage. The words echoed in Hans mind, the sting of Lukas's taunts cutting deeper than any physical blow.

CHAPTER 18

Scrambling for Cash

The sun had barely risen over Zurich, casting long shadows across the cobblestone streets. Hans Kaller walked with a determined stride, his heart pounding not just from anxiety, but from a fierce resolve. The memories of Anna and Lukas, together in their betrayal, haunted him, pushing him towards an unimaginable decision. He could see no other way out. Both of them had to go. They had left him no choice.

Hans knew the path he had chosen required more money, money that he did not have. But desperation breeds ingenuity. Clutching his coat tightly around him, Hans navigated through the narrow back alleys of Zurich, areas he had once avoided in his days of success and literary fame. Now, they seemed like the only places where he could find what he needed.

He stopped in front of a small, nondescript shop with a faded sign hanging above the door. The windows were filthy, and the faint smell of dampness and decay came out each time the door swung open. Hans took a deep breath and stepped inside.

The shopkeeper, a thin man with a cunning face, looked up from behind the counter, his eyes narrowing as he appraised Hans. Without a word, Hans reached into his bag and pulled out his prized possession: an old, yet meticulously maintained Hermes typewriter. It had been his companion through countless nights of inspiration and ingenuity, the instrument of his greatest works. He remembered writing his most famous novel, *The Zurich Shadows* on this very typewriter. But now, it was a memory of the past he could no longer relate to.

The shopkeeper's eyes gleamed with interest as Hans placed the expensive Hermes typewriter on the counter. "How much?" Hans asked, his voice steady but his hands trembling.

The shopkeeper examined the typewriter with expert hands, pressing the keys and listening to the smooth click. "Two hundred francs," he said finally, his tone betraying a hint of greed.

Hans knew he was being lowballed, but he didn't have the luxury of time to haggle. He nodded curtly. The shopkeeper counted out the money, and Hans shoved it into his coat pocket, feeling a pang of sorrow as he left his most prized possession behind.

Next, he made his way to a small pawnshop at the edge of the district. The bell above the door jingled as he entered, and a stout woman behind the counter looked up, her eyes narrowing in suspicion. Hans didn't wait for her to speak. He placed his expensive Rolex watch and a few pieces of jewellery on the counter—gifts from Anna and his friends during happier times.

The woman scrutinised the items with a practised eye. "What do you need?" she asked, her voice sharp.

"Money, of course," Hans replied. "How much can you give me for these?"

She hesitated for a moment, then nodded. "Three thousand francs."

Hans felt his heart sink. It wasn't enough. He needed more. But he had nothing else to offer. He took the money, barely muttering his thanks before rushing out into the street.

During the next few days, Hans sold and pawned the remaining valuables from his home, sold them one by one in the dingy bylanes of Zurich and hungrily collected money that he desperately needed to push his plan forward.

He even sold his wedding ring in a fit of desperation, to a jeweller he knew beforehand, and that gave him enough cash to take his plans to fruition.

Soon, it would be over, Hans thought. Soon, he would be free.

CHAPTER 19

Pulling the Trigger

The confrontation with Lukas and Anna had left Hans feeling more humiliated and enraged than ever. The weight of his suspicions was pressing heavily upon him. Hans always prided himself on being a rational man, but the thought of Anna's betrayal shattered his sanity. Memories of their happier times further pained Hans — her laughter, the gentle touch of her hand, and the dreams they once shared.

Can he still confront her, seek counseling, or perhaps rekindle the fading spark? Hans weighed the options in front of him. For a moment it felt that all is not lost for their marriage.

Yet, the image of Lukas intruding upon their sacred bond was an red line. The pain of her deceit overshadowed the love that once was between them. With a deep, shuddering breath, Hans felt a cold resolve solidify within him. The path of no return was here, and Hans now chose to walk it.

It was time to pull the trigger and set his plan into motion. He thought of eliminating Lukas along with Anna, as he felt Lukas was equally responsible for his current condition.

Hans sat in his dimly lit study, the weight of the decision pressing heavily on him. The piece of paper with the contact details of the Albanian contract killer lay in front of him. He took a deep breath, picked up his phone, and dialled the number. The line rang twice before a rough voice answered.

"Yeah?"

"It's Hans," he said, his voice steady. "We met a few nights ago. I need to move forward with our plan."

There was a pause on the other end before the voice responded. "Alright. What do you have in mind?"

Hans swallowed hard, steeling himself for what he was about to say. "I want Anna eliminated. And I need to know the cost of eliminating Lukas as well."

The man on the other end chuckled darkly. "You're not messing around, are you? Alright, let's talk specifics. Two murders will cost more money than what we agreed upon, you understand right?"

Hans leaned back in his chair, the leather creaking under his weight. "Money is not an issue. I want this done right."

"Good to know. For Anna, we have a few options. Quick and clean, like a car accident or poisoning. If you want something more personal and painful, the price goes up. Stabbing, strangulation—that sort of thing will cost you fifteen to twenty grand, depending on the details."

Hans felt a shiver run down his spine at the cold, clinical way the man spoke about murder. "What about Lukas?"

"Same pricing structure applies. If you want both done, we can offer a package deal. Twenty-five grand for quick and clean, Thirty-five grand for more painful methods."

Hans took a deep breath, his mind racing. "Tell me more about the painful methods for Anna. I want her to suffer."

The man on the other end chuckled, as he seemed to sense Hans' desperation.

"Stabbing is a good option. It's up close and personal, and it sends a strong message. Multiple wounds, slow and painful. Strangulation is also effective—watching the life drain from her eyes gives you a sense of control."

Hans closed his eyes, imagining the scenes described to him. "And how soon can this be done?"

"Once we receive the address, we can move quickly. A few days to set everything up. We'll make it look like a robbery gone wrong, if you prefer."

Hans nodded, though the man couldn't see him. "Alright. I'll wire the rest of the money today. Make it look like a robbery. And for Lukas... quick and clean. An accident."

"You got it. I'll send you the details for the wire transfer. Once we have the money, we'll take care of the rest."

Hans ended the call, his hands trembling. The finality of his decision settled over him, a cold, heavy weight. He knew there was no turning back now. The wheels were in motion, and soon, Anna and Lukas would be out of his life forever.

He made the wire transfer as instructed, his mind numb as he input the details. The money left his account, emptying his account completely and with it, any hope of redemption. He had nearly sold all his valuables, and all his prized possessions now belonged to Zurich's pawn shops. Hans sat back in his chair, staring at the screen, the reality of his actions sinking in.

The days that followed were a blur. Hans went through the motions of his daily life, his mind consumed by the impending acts of violence. Each night, he lay awake, haunted by the images of what was to come. The darkness within him grew, fueled by his anger and desire for revenge.

Hans waited patiently for his phone to ring.

CHAPTER 20

The First Attempt

Anna sat in the living room of her new beautiful house. This beautiful new house in Zurich's posh Riesbach area gave her immense freedom from Hans' toxic presence and gave her freedom to spend more time with the love of her life, Lukas.

But right now she was a tad worried. Sipping a cup of jasmine tea, she was trying to calm her nerves. Something was off. She'd had an eerie feeling she couldn't just shake.

After Hans caught her and Lukas in their intimate moments, Anna was worried that something bad might happen. She constantly used to worry about Hans' reaction. Will he let it go and move on, or will he do something nastier? The sharp wind outside matched her inner turmoil, the wind and rain a perfect reflection of her unsettled mind.

She was lost in thought when she heard a noise from the back of the house. It was faint at first, but then she heard it again—a creak, followed by a muffled thud. Her heart rate quickened as she set her cup down and stood up, straining to hear over the storm.

Anna moved cautiously towards the noise, her senses on high alert. She reached the hallway, peering into the darkness. The dim light from the living room cast long shadows, making it difficult to see. She took a deep breath, steeling herself as she moved forward.

Suddenly, a strong figure lunged at her from the darkness, a knife glinting in the faint light. At first, Anna recoiled in fear, and a sharp scream left her lips.

Soon, Anna reacted instinctively, her hands coming up to block the attack. She felt a sharp pain in her arm as the blade grazed her, but she didn't stop. She fought back with all her strength, adrenaline fueling her movements.

The man started choking Anna, as she blocked his other hand with her full strength. Anna's heart pounded with fear as the intruder's cold hands tightened around her neck. She gasped for breath, and her vision started blurring as she fought to stay conscious.

Summoning every ounce of her strength, she grabbed his wrist. Her nails were digging into his skin as she tried to push his grip loose. Desperation fueled her movements, with her muscles straining as she blocked his other hand, preventing him from reaching for the knife. Her whole life flashed before her, as she lay on the floor in her own home, underpinned by a stranger and struggled desperately for survival.

The room was a chaotic whirl of sounds and shadows, their struggle punctuated by the harsh rasp of her laboured breathing and the man's grunts of exertion. Anna's thoughts raced, searching for any means of escape. She twisted her body, trying to create enough leverage to break free.

Her legs kicked out, knocking over a nearby table, sending a lamp crashing to the floor. The sudden noise startled the intruder, giving Anna a fleeting moment of advantage. She managed to push him back slightly, just enough to draw a ragged breath and prepare for the next desperate move.

The intruder was strong, but Anna's fear and determination gave her an edge. She managed to push him back, but he recovered quickly, coming at her again.

They struggled, the knife flashing between them as they grappled. Anna felt the cold steel bite into her skin again, but she ignored the pain, focusing on survival.

She screamed and dodged, but he was strong and relentless. They struggled fiercely, their bodies crashing into furniture and toppling over all the items in the room.

Anna's survival instinct kicked in, and she fought back with every ounce of strength she had, adrenaline coursing through her veins.

The struggle was intense, the goon's strength overpowering, but Anna's determination was unwavering. She managed to grab a heavy vase and smash it against his head, momentarily dazing him.

Seizing the opportunity, she pushed him away and scrambled to her feet, only to be grabbed again. The knife slashed through the air, scratching her shoulder and letting out a splash of blood, as they continued to wrestle.

Despite the odds, Anna's will to live fueled her efforts, and with a final burst of energy, Anna shoved the intruder hard. He stumbled, losing his balance on the dishevelled floor.

She watched in horror as he fell backwards, tumbling down the stairs. The sickening sound of his body hitting the steps echoed through the house, followed by a final, bone-crunching thud.

Anna stood frozen, her face contorted with fear and her breath coming in ragged gasps. She looked down at the crumpled figure at the bottom of the stairs, with her mind struggling to process what had just happened. The knife lay a few feet away, glinting ominously in the dim light.

Anna's clothes were torn and tattered from the violent struggle, hanging in shreds around her bruised and battered body. Her arms and legs bore deep purple bruises, and multiple gashes on her body trickled blood down her face and arms.

Each breath she took was laboured, as her body was aching from the relentless assault. Despite the pain and the disarray, her eyes burned with the fierce determination that had kept her alive. The physical toll was immense, but the spark of survival still shone brightly in her battered form.

She moved slowly, her body aching from the struggle. Her arm throbbed where the knife had cut her, blood seeping through her sleeve. She reached for her phone with trembling hands, and dialled 112, the police emergency helpline.

"There's been an accident," she managed to say, while sobbing quietly. "Someone broke into my house... I think he's dead."

Hans waited anxiously in his study, the hours ticking by with agonising slowness. The plan was in motion, and soon, he would be free of Anna and Lukas forever. The anticipation was almost unbearable, the tension twisting in his gut like a knife.

He replayed the details of the plan in his mind, each step meticulously designed to ensure success. Yet, despite his careful planning, a nagging doubt lingered at the back of his mind.

The night was dark and stormy, the wind howling outside as rain battered against the windows. Hans sat in his chair, staring at the phone, waiting for the call that would confirm the deed was done.

The minutes dragged on, each one an eternity. Finally, the phone rang, the sound jarring in the silence. Hans picked it up, his heart pounding in his chest.

"Attack happened tonight, as planned," the rough voice on the other end.

Hans let out a breath he hadn't realised he was holding. "Both of them?" he asked, his voice trembling slightly.

"Not exactly," the man replied, his tone grim. "There was a problem."

Hans's heart skipped a beat. "What do you mean, a problem?"

The man sighed. "The guy we sent for Anna... he didn't make it."

Hans felt a chill run down his spine. "What happened?"

"We planned it perfectly. He was supposed to get in, knife her, and make it look like a robbery gone wrong. But it didn't go as planned. Your wife put up a tough fight."

Hans's mind raced, imagining the scene. "What do you mean? How did she—?"

"He underestimated her," the man cut in. "She fought back harder than he expected. In the struggle, she managed to push him, and he fell down the stairs. Broke his neck on impact."

Hans felt a wave of nausea wash over him. "And Anna?"

"She's alive. Badly bruised, but alive. The police are investigating it as a home invasion gone wrong, just like we planned. But she survived."

Hans closed his eyes with exertion, the mix of emotions overwhelming him.

"So what now?"

"We need to regroup. It's going to be harder to get to her now. She'll be on high alert. But we can still do it. It will just take some more planning."

Hans hung up the phone, and his mind was spinning hard. The failed attempt left him reeling and jaded. He had come so close to being free of Anna, but his bad luck was not letting him succeed.

Hans realised that his situation was getting worse.

CHAPTER 21

The Dangerous Drive

The failed attempt on Anna's life left Hans feeling more desperate and unhinged than ever. The rage and humiliation he had felt watching Lukas and Anna making love together was turning into a dark obsession.

He knew he had to try again. The first failure had only strengthened his resolve. He would not let Anna escape his grasp.

Hans sat in his study, dialling the Albanian goon's number once more. The voice on the other end was tense, anticipating the fallout from the failed attempt.

"It is Hans. We need to try again," he said, his voice cold and determined.

The rough voice sighed. "We can do that, but it'll be more difficult now. She will be on high alert."

"I don't care. It has to be done," Hans insisted.

"Alright," the man replied. "We'll plan another attempt. This time, we'll use a different method—something less direct but just as effective."

Hans felt a twisted sense of satisfaction. "What's the plan?"

"We'll stage a car accident. We'll tamper with the brakes on her car. When she drives, it will look like she lost control of the car. Simple, clean, and effective."

Hans nodded. "Do it."

The man agreed, and they hung up. Hans leaned back in his chair, a dark smile playing on his lips.

Anna had been on edge since the break-in. She couldn't shake the feeling of being watched, of danger lurking around every corner. She had installed new locks and a security system for her new home, but it did little to ease her mind. Every noise, every shadow, set her heart racing.

Next morning, as she got into her car to head to work, she felt a sense of unease. She dismissed it as paranoia, starting the engine and pulling out of the driveway. She tried to focus on the road ahead, but her mind kept drifting back to the night of the attack.

The busy streets of Zurich, usually a familiar comfort, now seemed to close in around her as she navigated through the heavy traffic.

As she accelerated, she felt something amiss – the brakes were not responding as they should. Panic surged through her, but she forced herself to stay calm, gripping the steering wheel tightly as she swerved hard to avoid hitting a pedestrian crossing the street.

The car raced forward uncontrollably, and Anna's heart pounded in her chest. She narrowly missed a collision with a delivery van, the sound of its blaring horn echoing in her ears. The brakes were definitely not working, and her car was cruising at a very high speed!

Her mind raced as fast as the car, calculating every move to avoid disaster. She honked frantically, weaving through side lanes, narrowly avoiding vehicles and cyclists. The cityscape blurred around her, each collision she missed was a razor-thin escape from impending catastrophe.

Fear and adrenaline surged through her as she jumped the car through a wide intersection, barely avoiding an incoming tram. For a moment, she thought she was going to die a crushing death under the tram.

Her hands ached from gripping the wheel so tightly, and her knuckles were white now. She glanced at the terrified faces of other drivers, her own fear mirrored in their eyes.

With each second the car's speed was increasing. Anna desperately fought to control her car. She swerved the car hard right to avoid a collision with a motorbike up front, and the bike rider's yell at her got lost in the chaos of the heavy traffic.

Desperation took hold as she spotted an upcoming roundabout. With no other choice, Anna turned the wheel hard, sending the car into a complete wild spin. Tires screeched like crazy, and the car slid dangerously close to a canal before it finally slowed, scraping to a halt as it crashed against a traffic barrier.

Completely shaken but unharmed, Anna took a deep breath, her mind reeling from the near misses and the horrifying realisation of what could have just happened.

She sat there, trembling, her breath coming in short gasps. Her mind raced with the implications. This was not a simple accident. Someone had tampered with her car, and she had barely escaped with her life.

Hans waited anxiously for news of the accident, his mind filled with lusty anticipation. The call came later that day.

"It didn't work," the rough Albanian voice said, frustration evident in his tone. "She survived. She managed to stop the car before it crashed."

Hans felt a surge of anger. "How is that possible? You said it would work."

"It should have," the man replied. "But she got lucky. We'll need to try something else."

Hans clenched his fists, his rage threatening to overwhelm him. "No more mistakes. Do whatever it takes. I want her dead, do you understand?"

The man sighed. "We will regroup and come up with a new plan. But it will take time. We cannot afford to mess up again."

Hans ended the call, his mind racing. The failed attempts were driving him to the brink.

Days turned into weeks, and Anna lived in a constant state of fear. The police investigation into the break-in and the car tampering yielded few leads. She felt trapped, with her beautiful home no longer a peaceful sanctuary but became a high security prison for her. Lukas was the only bright light in her life, and she began to cherish her time with Lukas even more.

Hans, meanwhile, grew more desperate. The failed attempts had only deepened his obsession. He reached out to the Albanian boss once more, determined to see his plan through.

"We need a new plan, and quick." Hans said, his voice filled with frustration.

The man on the other end was silent for a moment before responding. "We will plan something different this time. Something dark and dangerous, that we have not tried earlier. Are you ok with a painful death for your lovely wife?" he asked with a devious smile, that Hans could well sense over the line.

Hans agreed, his mind filled with visions of Anna's final moments. He could not afford to wait any longer. He needed to end this painful episode in his life, and end this fast. He had paid a lot of money to the Albanian gang that he could barely afford, and now these repeated failures were taking a toll on his mental state.

CHAPTER 22

The Darkened Streets

Hans was growing increasingly desperate. The failed attempts on Anna's life had only heightened his determination to see her eliminated. He reached out to his Albanian contact once more, ready to discuss yet another plan.

This time, it needed to be something different, something unexpected.

The rough Albanian voice on the other end of the line was as calm and collected as ever. "We need to change our approach," he said. "We'll use a different method this time, something that will catch her off guard."

Hans listened intently, his mind racing. "What do you have in mind?"

"Eve-teasing!" the man replied. "We will stage an attack in a dark part of town. She will be alone and vulnerable, and we will make it look like a random assault. It will be brutal, but it won't raise too many suspicions."

Hans felt a shiver run down his spine. "Do it. But make sure it is done right. I want her dead at any cost. No more failures this time please."

The man agreed, and they hung up. Hans's mind was filled with visions of the upcoming attack. He could almost see Anna's terror, her helplessness. It filled him with a twisted sense of satisfaction. This time, he was sure the gang would succeed.

Anna had been trying to regain some sense of normalcy in her life, despite the recent events that had left her shaken. She had resumed her work routine, hoping that the familiarity of daily humdrum would help her feel safer.

That evening, she attended a late meeting with a client at her art gallery, and as she left, she felt a sense of unease. The weather was unusually cold as it was drizzling a bit.

She pulled her coat tighter around her as she walked, her footsteps echoing in the deserted streets. She had parked her car a few blocks away, and she was regretting her decision to walk alone in this wet weather. The darkened alleyways and shadowy corners seemed more menacing than usual. She kept her head down, her pace quickening as she neared a particularly isolated part of town.

Suddenly, she heard multiple footsteps behind her, with the chorus growing louder and closer. Her heart pounded in her chest as she turned to look, her eyes widening in fear. Three men emerged from the shadows, their faces obscured by the darkness. They moved in quickly, and surrounded her before she could react.

"Hey there, pretty lady," one of them sneered, his voice dripping with malice. "Out all alone at this hour? That's not very smart for a sexy girl like you."

Anna's breath caught in her throat as she backed away, her mind racing. "Please, just leave me alone," she managed to say, her voice trembling.

The men laughed, their intentions clear. "Oh, we are just getting started," another one said, stepping closer. He reached out, grabbing her arm with a rough grip.

Anna struggled, trying to pull away, but the men were too strong. They dragged her deep inside a dark lane and pushed her against the wall, their hands groping her body and tearing her clothes.

She screamed, the sound echoing through the empty streets, but there was no one around to hear her cries for help. The ongoing drizzle, loud and cold winds and the occasional fast traffic downed her cries for help.

"Shut her up," one of the men growled, covering her mouth with his hand. Anna's eyes widened with terror as she again tried to scream, her voice now muffled by his strong grip.

One of the men slapped her a few times on her face to soften her up. Tears of pain and humiliation rolled down Anna's eyes.

The leader of the group pinned her arms above her head, his ugly face inches from hers. "You are gonna regret coming out tonight, honey," he hissed, his breath hot against her skin.

Tears streamed down Anna's cheeks as she struggled against them, her mind filled with panic and terror. She kicked and thrashed, trying to break free, but it only seemed to amuse them.

The men laughed, their hands roaming her body, tearing at her clothes. Her coat was lost in the mele earlier. The sound of soft fabric of Anna's dress ripping apart filled the air as they shredded her blouse, exposing her nipples to the cold night air.

One strong palm cupped her breast, as one the men toyed with and twisted her nipples. She closed her eyes as she could not bear the humiliation of being topless in front of three strange men.

The three men laughed menacingly, taking turns. With multiple hands freely roaming on her body, kissing and biting at her skin, and tearing at her modesty, Anne felt she was surrounded by a pack of hungry wolves.

One of the men forced his distasteful tongue deep inside her mouth, and she immediately got repulsed by the taste of his filthy saliva entering her mouth.

The leader slowly started pushing her remaining dress down. He was rubbing his own manhood and was gently preparing himself for the final assault. The other two men licked their lips, awaiting their turn at destroying this pretty damsel.

Anna felt that she would die a painful death today.

The three men overcome with their lust and the sight of Anna's naked body became a bit careless and confident. She was pinned to the wall, almost naked, and they felt now was the time to rejoice and enjoy their evening.

Anna sensed her chance. In a moment of courage, Anna's survival instincts kicked in. She managed to twist her body, bringing her knee up and hit hard into the leader's now exposed manhood.

He let out a deep pained grunt, his grip loosening just enough for her to break free. She pushed him away hard, her heart racing as she made a mad run for freedom. The leader fell on the other two men, both busy caressing their manhoods with their pants down their knees.

The other two men were momentarily stunned, but they quickly recovered. The three lost some time in pulling their pants up, and started chasing after her. Anna's breath came in ragged gasps as she ran with madness, with her feet pounding against the pavement. She lost her shoe to gain pace and kept running barefoot and almost-naked on the wet-cold streets of Zurich.

She could hear their footsteps approaching behind her, and their sounds filling her heart with dread and fear. She gathered the last reserves of strength from deep within herself, and made a frantic, final dash for freedom.

She took a sharp left turn at the corner, and spotted a Avec 24X7 convenience store at the end of the street. The lights on the store were on, and she could see the silhouette of the store clerk inside. Summoning every ounce of her last remaining strength, she sprinted towards the store, her vision getting blurred with tears.

Anna burst through the glass door, and collapsed onto the store floor. The clerk looked up in shock, and rushed to her side. "Are you okay? What happened?"

"They... they tried to rape me," Anna sobbed, her body shaking. "Please, call the police."

The clerk nodded, grabbed the phone and dialled 112. Anna lay on the floor, her body bruised and battered, her clothes in complete tatters, but she was relieved to be alive. The fear slowly ebbed away, leaving her exhausted and breathless.

She pulled a rug to cover her modesty, as store customers started gathering around her.

Hans waited anxiously for news of the planned attack. He paced up and down his study, with his mind filled with dark anticipation. When the call finally came, his heart pounded in his chest.

"It did not work," the rough voice said, frustration evident in his tone. "The bitch got away, again."

Hans felt a surge of anger and helplessness. "How could you let that happen?"

"She fought back. Got away before we could finish the job. The Federal police are involved now. We need to back off for a while."

Hans clenched his fists, his rage and desperation threatening to overwhelm him. He almost begged in desperation, "Finish her please. I paid you everything I had. Do whatever it takes, but you need to kill her."

"We will regroup and come up with a new plan. But it will take time now. We cannot risk another attempt right away. The Feds are involved now."

Hans hung up, his mind seething with anger. The failed attempts were driving him mad. He couldn't let Anna slip through his fingers.

"I have to personally carry out Anna's murder," Hans thought, "The Albanians are a bunch of bullshit people."

Anna sat in her apartment, the cruel events of the night replaying in her mind. She felt a mix of fear and relief. The attack had been brutal, but she had survived. She knew she couldn't let her guard down.

Someone really wanted her dead. Was it Hans, or was it a past disgruntled employee? Was it an art deal gone wrong? She did deal with a lot of rich and powerful people and she didn't know who was after her life. Was it a series of unconnected events? Her head started spinning in the myriads of dark possibilities.

The Swiss federal police had promised to investigate, but Anna felt a growing sense of paranoia. She couldn't trust anyone now.

She needed to protect herself, and to be ready for whatever came next. The struggle for survival was far from over, and Anna knew she had to be strong.

As she looked out the window, with the city lights twinkling in the distance, Anna made a silent vow. She would not let her fear control her. She would fight back, no matter what it takes. She would find a way to survive, to uncover the truth, and to reclaim her life.

Anna promised herself that she would not allow the darkness that has invaded her life to destroy her.

She knew Lukas loved her, and this gave her immense strength.

CHAPTER 23

Respite in the Swiss Countryside

Anna sat in her apartment, the events of the past weeks weighing heavily on her mind. The recent attack had left her shaken and paranoid. She knew she needed a break, a chance to escape the suffocating fear that had taken hold of her life.

It was Lukas who suggested the weekend getaway, offering her a glimmer of hope in the midst of darkness. He was equally shocked at the sudden, dark turn of events in recent days.

"We need to get out of here, Anna," Lukas said, his voice gentle but firm. "A change of scenery will do you good. Let's go to the countryside for a few days. It'll be safe, and you can finally relax."

Anna hesitated, the thought of leaving the city was both tempting and frightening for her. But Lukas's reassuring presence gave her the courage she needed. She nodded, a small smile appearing at her lips. "Alright, let's go for it. I can really use a little break."

The next morning, they packed their bags and set off for the Swiss countryside. The drive was long, but the beauty of the landscape slowly began to soothe Anna's frayed nerves.

They hired a beautiful open-top convertible car for this ride, as Anna's car was completely smashed in the brake-fail accident.

The bustling city streets gave way to rolling hills and lush green meadows, the air growing fresher with each passing mile. The sight of snow-capped mountains in the distance filled her with a sense of peace she hadn't felt in weeks.

Lukas drove with one hand on the wheel, his other hand resting on Anna's knee, a comforting presence. "You're going to love it out here," he said, glancing over at her with a warm smile. "It's the perfect place to unwind."

Anna looked out the window, her heart swelling with gratitude. The countryside was like a painting, each scene more beautiful than the last. The fresh air breeze over the open top was a refreshing change from the fear and suffocation she felt over the past couple of weeks.

She watched as pretty villages passed by, their charming houses nestled among fields of wildflowers.

They arrived at a cosy cottage nestled at the edge of a forest, its stone walls and thatched roof giving it a fairytale-like charm. Lukas helped Anna out of the car, their fingers intertwining as they walked up the path. The air was filled with the scent of pine and blooming flowers, a gentle breeze rustling the leaves.

Inside, the cottage was warm and inviting, and Lukas expertly set the cosy, warm fire in the elegant fireplace. Anna set their bags down and sank into the plush armchair. The tension in her shoulders felt slowly melting away. Lukas walked over to her, and brushed a strand of hair away from her tired face.

"How are you feeling?" he asked softly, his eyes filled with concern.

Anna smiled up at him, her heart swelling with affection. "Better. This place is amazing, Lukas. Thank you."

Lukas leaned down, pressing a gentle kiss to her forehead. "Anything for you, Anna. You deserve to feel safe and happy."

The next few days were a blissful escape from reality. Lukas and Anna spent their mornings exploring the countryside, hiking through dense forests and meandering along crystal-clear streams. The beauty of nature surrounded them, each moment a reminder of the simple joys of life.

One afternoon, they walked to a nearby private garden, with its grass soft and inviting. They lay down side by side, as the sky was turning a brilliant shade of blue overhead. Lukas turned to Anna, his eyes sparkling with mischief.

"Do you remember the last time we came out here together?" he asked, a playful grin tugging at his lips.

Anna laughed, the sound of her laughter was like music to Lukas's ears. "How could I forget? You tried to impress me by climbing that tree and ended up falling into the stream."

Lukas chuckled, his laughter warm and genuine. "I was trying to get the perfect view. And hey, it worked, didn't it? You've been hooked on me ever since."

Anna rolled her eyes, but her smile was radiant. "You are impossible, Lukas."

They shared a tender kiss, with the world around them fading into the background. For the first time in weeks, Anna felt truly at peace.

As the sun set, casting a golden glow over the landscape, Lukas led Anna back to the cottage. He had planned a special dinner, as he wanted to make their time together unforgettable. The dining table was set with candles and flowers, the soft light creating a romantic ambiance.

They shared a delicious meal, and the conversation flew easily between them. Lukas was attentive and loving, and his presence was a healing balm to Anna's wounded spirit. After dinner, they moved to the living room. The fire from the fireplace was casting a warm glow over their faces.

Lukas pulled Anna into his lap, his arms wrapping around her protectively. "I want you to know that I am here for you, no matter what," he murmured, his lips brushing against her ear. "We will get through this together."

Anna snuggled closer to him, her heart filled with gratitude and love. "Thank you, Lukas. I don't know what I would do without you."

They spent the rest of the evening making love to each other. In the afterglow of sex, they wrapped themselves in each other's arms, with the crackling fire and gentle sounds of the countryside lulling them into a sense of security. The outside world and its dangers felt a million miles away, and for the first time in a long while, Anna felt a lot of hope for the future.

Over the next few days, Lukas and Anna continued to explore the beauty of the Swiss countryside. They visited nearby charming villages, sampled local delicacies, and spent lazy afternoons lounging by the lake. Each moment was a step towards healing, the love and connection between them growing stronger.

One evening, as they watched the sunset from a hilltop, Lukas turned to Anna, his expression serious. "You know, we can't stay here forever. Eventually, we'll have to go back and face whatever is waiting for us."

Anna nodded, her heart heavy with the truth of his words. "I know. But this time away has given me the strength I needed. I'm ready to face whatever comes, as long as I have you by my side."

Lukas took her hand, squeezing it gently. "You're not alone, Anna. We'll face it together, and we'll come out stronger."

With Lukas by her side, Anna knew she could face any challenge and still win!

CHAPTER 24
Uncovering the Truth

The return to the city was bittersweet for Anna and Lukas. The serenity of the Swiss countryside had given them a reprieve from the turmoil, but now they had to face the grim reality of the situation.

For Lukas, the past days of reflection had given rise to a growing suspicion about Hans. The three failed attempts on Anna's life felt too targeted, too personal. He couldn't shake the feeling that Hans was behind it all.

One evening, as they settled back into Anna's new beautiful home, Lukas broached the subject with Anna.

"Anna, I've been thinking a lot about everything that's happened," Lukas began, his tone serious. "The attacks, the car tampering... it all feels too coordinated to be a coincidence."

Anna looked at him, her eyes filled with concern. "What are you saying, Lukas?"

Lukas took a deep breath. "I think Hans might be behind this. He has the motive, and he's capable of planning something like this. We need to talk to someone, maybe get the police involved."

Anna's eyes widened in shock, but as she considered Lukas's words, she realised he might be right. "But... What if you're wrong? What if he isn't involved?"

Lukas took her hand, his grip reassuring. "Then we'll find out for sure. But we can't ignore the possibility. You deserve to be safe, Anna."

Anna nodded slowly. "You're right. We need to talk to the police." The more that Anna considered the possibility of Hans' involvement, the more she realised that Lukas was not very far from the truth.

The next day, Lukas and Anna made their way to the local police station. The atmosphere was tense as they approached the front desk. Lukas asked to speak with the police chief, explaining that they had important information about the recent attacks on Anna's life.

They were ushered into a small, barely furnished office where Chief Inspector Martin Mueller, a seasoned officer with a reputation for solid detective work, awaited them. He stood up, extending a hand in greeting.

"Mr. Lukas, Ms. Anna, please have a seat," Chief Mueller said, his tone professional but kind. "I understand you have some concerns about the recent incidents."

Lukas nodded, his expression serious. "Yes, Chief Mueller. We believe there's more to these attacks than random acts of violence. We think Anna's estranged husband, Hans, might be involved."

Chief Mueller raised an eyebrow, his interest piqued. "That's a serious accusation. Can you explain why you suspect Mr. Hans?"

Lukas took a deep breath, recounting the events leading up to their suspicions. "There have been several attempts on Anna's life, all of which seem too well-planned to be random. First, there was a break-in at her house, then her car brakes were tampered with, and most recently, she was brutally attacked in the street. Hans has the motive. He's been angry and resentful since their separation."

Anna nodded, her voice trembling slightly as she spoke. "Hans always had a strong temper. And with everything that's happened... it just makes sense that he could be behind it."

Chief Mueller listened intently, his expression thoughtful. "These are serious allegations. If Hans is involved, we need concrete evidence. Have you noticed any other suspicious behaviour from him?"

Lukas nodded. "He's been unusually interested in Anna's life. He shows up at places where she is, even though they're not supposed to be in contact. It's almost like he's keeping tabs on her movement."

Chief Mueller leaned back in his chair, considering their words. "Alright. We'll open an investigation. We'll start by monitoring Hans' activities and look into his connections. If he's involved, we will definitely find the proof we need."

Anna felt a wave of relief wash over her. "Thank you, Chief Mueller. I just want this nightmare to be over."

Chief Mueller nodded, his expression firm and resolute. "We'll do everything we can to ensure your safety, Ms. Anna. In the meantime, please take extra precautions. Avoid being alone and stay in well-lit, populated areas."

As they left the police station, Anna and Lukas felt a glimmer of hope. The police were now involved, and the truth would eventually come to light. They returned home, determined to support each other through the challenges ahead.

Chief Mueller wasted no time in launching the investigation. He assigned a team of detectives to monitor Hans's movements and check his background. They discreetly followed him, tracking his daily activities and looking for any signs of suspicious behaviour.

At the same time, Mueller instructed his team to re-examine the previous incidents with fresh eyes. They revisited the scene of the break-in, scrutinised the evidence from the car tampering, and interviewed witnesses from the store, the night Anna was attacked.

Each piece of the puzzle was carefully analysed, with the aim of building a case against Hans if he was indeed guilty. As the days passed, the detectives began to uncover small but significant clues. Hans was seen meeting with shady individuals in secluded locations, and his behaviour was secretive and cautious. He visited pawn shops, bars and roamed around Zurich's dark alleys, like a man possessed. He was no longer the famous author they thought he was.

They intercepted Hans' phone calls and messages that hinted at orchestrating something sinister, though the finer details were still unclear.

One evening, as the detectives observed Hans from a distance, they saw him exchange an envelope with a known Albanian gangster. The meeting was brief, but it confirmed their suspicions that Hans was involved in some kind of illegal activity. They documented everything, building a dossier of evidence.

A week later, Chief Mueller called Lukas and Anna back to the station. They sat in the same small office, their hearts pounding with anticipation.

"We have made some progress," Chief Mueller began, his tone serious. "Our investigation has uncovered several suspicious activities linked to Hans. We have documented Hans' meetings with known criminals, seen him at shady places that he routinely visits and intercepted communications that suggest he might be planning something harmful."

Anna's breath caught in her throat. "So it's true? Hans is behind this?"

Chief Mueller nodded. "It appears so. We don't have enough evidence for an arrest yet, but we're getting close. We need to catch him in the act or find more concrete evidence."

Lukas squeezed Anna's hand, his expression determined. "What can we do to help?"

Chief Mueller leaned forward, his gaze intense. "We need to continue monitoring him closely. Any information you can provide, no matter how small, could be crucial. And we need you both to be vigilant. If you notice anything unusual, let us know immediately."

Anna nodded, her resolve strengthening. "We will. Thank you, Chief Mueller."

As they left the station, Lukas and Anna felt a renewed sense of determination. The investigation was progressing, and they were closer to uncovering the truth. With the police on their side, they knew they had a fighting chance.

Back at their apartment, Lukas and Anna discussed their next steps. They decided to install additional security measures and avoid public places as much as possible. Lukas made sure to stay by Anna's side, and his presence was a constant source of comfort and strength for Anna.

Days turned into weeks, as the police investigation continued. The tension was palpable, but so was their determination to see justice served. Each day brought them closer to the truth, and they held onto the hope that soon, the nightmare would soon end.

Hans, unaware that he was being watched, continued with his plans. But the walls were closing in on him, and it was only a matter of time before his actions caught up with him.

The police were relentless, and with Lukas and Anna's help, they were determined to ensure that justice was served. As the investigation progressed, Anna and Lukas grew closer, their bond strengthened by the challenges they faced. They knew the road ahead would be difficult, but they were ready to face it together. The darkness that had invaded their lives was beginning to lift, and they were determined to emerge stronger and more resilient than ever.

The battle for justice was far from over, but with each step forward, they knew they were closer to victory. The truth would prevail, and Hans would face the consequences of his actions, if he is guilty.

Anna and Lukas vowed to fight together, guided by their endless love for each other, which was getting stronger by the day.

CHAPTER 25

Cat and Mouse Game

Hans Kaller sat in a dark corner of a dingy café, as the dim light cast shadows on his tensed face. He nursed a lukewarm cup of coffee, his hands trembling slightly as he took a sip. The events of the past few days had left him a wreck, his nerves were frayed and his mind was teetering on the edge of madness.

It all began with a phonc call from the Albanian mafia, a call that sent a deep sensation of fear inside his heart. The voice on the other end was cold and menacing. The mob delivered a stark warning that Police Chief Martin Mueller was now suspicious of his involvement in the attacks on Anna.

"Police are watching you, Hans," the voice had said. "They think you are behind the attacks on Anna. You need to be careful."

Hans had felt the floor drop out from under him. He knew Mueller well; the police chief was a tenacious investigator, not one to be easily dissuaded once he latched onto a suspect.

The thought of Mueller's sharp eyes and his relentless chase of criminals filled Hans with dread. He had to disappear, at least for a while, until things calmed down.

From that moment, Hans became a ghost in his own city. He avoided his house, fearful that the police might be watching his house, and was waiting to catch him. Instead, he roamed the streets of Zurich. Hans became a fugitive in his own mind, constantly looking over his shoulder.

The city that had once been his sanctuary now felt like a net of threats and hidden dangers. During the day, he roamed the crowded areas, and blended himself with the crowds of tourists and locals. He would sit in parks, pretending to read a newspaper while his eyes roving around, scanning for any sign of police surveillance.

At night, Zurich transformed into a city of shadows for Hans. The narrow, winding alleys of the Old Town, with their cobblestone streets and historical buildings, became a maze of potential hiding places. Hans would slip into these alleys, walk close to the dark walls, as his heart raced at every sound. The echo of his footsteps seemed loud and deafening to him in the quiet, and he would often stop, holding his breath, convinced that someone was following him.

The first night after the warning, Hans saw them. At first, it was a flash of a uniform in his peripheral vision. They were not just figments of his imagination. Mueller had set his men on him. He could feel the noose tightening, with each day a little closer to snapping around his neck. He took a side alley and kept running hard to get away from the uniformed men.

He found temporary refuge in the most unlikely places. An abandoned warehouse near the industrial district provided shelter one night. The next night, he slept on a bench in a secluded corner of the Chinese Garden, hidden among the dense trees. He was always on the move, never staying in one place for too long, as his mind became a whirlwind of fear and anxiety.

Hans' appearance deteriorated rapidly. His once neat and tidy clothes were now rumpled and dirty, his hair unkempt, and a shadow of stubble covered his hollow and hungry cheeks. He avoided looking at his reflection, unable to face the poor, haunted man he had become.

One evening, as the city was bathing in the soft glow of streetlights, Hans found himself near the Zurich Opera House. The elegant building, with its grand columns and statues, seemed to mock him. He watched as well-dressed and rich patrons filed in, their laughter and chatter a stark contrast to his silent torment.

He turned and walked away. He aimlessly wandered through the city. The silence of the night was oppressive, broken only by the occasional distant sound of a car or the faint murmur of late-night conversations appearing from open windows. He kept walking till he was able to walk no more and crashed on the sidewalk with tiredness.

Hans' paranoia grew with each passing day. He saw Mueller's face everywhere—in the stern expressions of tram conductors, the scrutinising gaze of shopkeepers, the casual glance of passersby. Every interaction felt like a potential trap, and every person was a possible police spy.

One night, he found himself in the Langstrasse area, known for its vibrant nightlife and cafes. The streets were alive with music and laughter, the air thick with the scents of various cuisines. Hans realised he was so hungry, but he had no money to buy any food. He moved through the crowd like a ghost, his eyes constantly scanning, and his mind running a riot of suspicion.

He ducked into a smoky bar, hoping to lose himself in the anonymity of the crowd. The dimly lit interior was filled with shady people, their faces blurred by the haze of cigarette smoke. Hans rummaged through his pocket to find a few francs and ordered a drink. His hands were shaking as he lifted the glass to his lips. He sat hidden in a corner, trying to blend in the darkness, but every sound, every movement, seemed scary, feeding his own growing paranoia.

At one point, he caught sight of a man in a dark suit, standing near the bar, his eyes fixed on Hans. Panic surged through him, and he bolted from his seat, pushing his way through the crowd and out into the night. He ran down the street, his heart pounding, convinced that Mueller's men were closing in on him.

He had to stay one step ahead. His mind raced as he moved through the city, plotting his next move, and calculating the odds of his survival. The once-familiar streets now felt like the twists and turns of a spider web designed to trap him.

Hans' nights were filled with restless sleep, if he managed to sleep at all. He would doze off in hidden corners, waking up at the slightest noise, his body tense and ready to run. His dreams were plagued by visions of police raids, and of being dragged away in handcuffs. He dreamt of Anna's face either twisted in evil betrayal or with ecstasy of her sex with Lukas. He envisioned Lukas loudly laughing at him, as he rammed his manhood deep inside Anna, in Hans' own bed.

During the day, he sought refuge in libraries and museums, places where he could sit quietly and try to gather his thoughts. The Kunsthaus art museum, with its vast collection of art, became a temporary sanctuary. He would sit in front of the paintings, trying to lose himself in the colours and forms, but his mind always returned to the same dark thoughts.

Next afternoon, as he wandered through the city, he found himself in the Lindenhof district, with its stunning views of the Limmat River and the old town. He sat on a bench, staring out at the city below, his mind a storm of fear and regret. The beauty of Zurich, with its mix of old and modern architecture, seemed like a cruel joke, a stark contrast to the chaos inside him.

An elderly woman, moving slowly, paused beside him and placed a five-franc note in his lap. Hans realised she had mistaken him for a beggar. Hungry and penniless, he decided to take the money and managed to utter a few words of thanks. She walked away, satisfied at her daily act of kindness and act of helping homeless people of Zurich.

In the evening, as the lights faded, Hans slipped into the Bahnhofstrasse, the bustling heart of Zurich's commercial district. The street, usually filled with shoppers and tourists, was quieter at this hour. He kept to the shadows, his eyes looking at the reflections in the shop windows. He saw a figure in a police uniform scanning the crowd, and his heart skipped a beat. He quickly turned down a side street, and started running.

Hans found himself in the Altstadt, Zurich's Old Town, its old lanes a dark maze of narrow alleys and hidden corners. He ducked into a small courtyard, pressing his back against the cold stone wall, his breath coming in short gasps. He could hear footsteps approaching, and his mind raced. He needed a plan to escape.

As the footsteps grew louder, Hans spotted an open door to a cellar. Without a second thought, he slipped inside, descending into the darkness. He held his breath, listening as the footsteps passed by, fading into the distance. He allowed himself a moment of relief, but he knew he couldn't stay long in the cold cellar.

Hans hid in the cold cellar for hours, the cold seeping into his bones, his mind racing with fear and paranoia. He thought of Anna, of Lukas, of his life and success that he had lost.

Hans knew he was running out of options. He knew he wouldn't be able to dodge Zurich police

forever. And he ran out of money to feed himself. He was hungry, wet and cold. He did not remember when was the last time he took a warm bath.

Tears streamed down his cheeks as he cried silently for a long time. Eventually, he decided to return to his house. If the police came and arrested him, so be it. He had tried hiding for many days, but he couldn't do it anymore. With tired steps and a bowed head, Hans walked back to the warmth of his home.

Hans decided to await his impending arrest.

CHAPTER 26

Darker Roleplay

Hans' mind was a storm of frustration and desperation. The failed attempts to eliminate Anna stared at him in his face, with each failure a reminder of his impotence. He waited for something to happen, but nothing was moving as per his plans. He hid at home for days, waiting for his inevitable arrest, but the Zurich police never showed up.

He needed an outlet, a way to reclaim the sense of power and control he had lost. His thoughts turned once again to Sofia and Nadia, the two women who had shared his darkest fantasies before. He needed them now more than ever. He rummaged through the house for any remaining cash and managed to find some.

Hans drove to District 5, the seedy part of Zurich where he had met Sofia and Nadia before. The memories of their last encounter fueled his desire, his need to reenact his fantasies growing stronger with each passing mile.

He gripped the steering wheel tightly as he navigated the bustling streets of Zurich. The evening sky was painted with hues of orange and purple, but Hans was oblivious to its beauty. His mind was set on the hotel room where he would play his games with Sophia and Nadia.

Inside, the air was thick with now familiar cigarette smoke and the low hum of conversation. Hans ran his eyes through the smoky interior, but could not spot Sophia and Nadia anywhere, and his heart sank.

He made his way to the bar counter, ordered a whiskey on the rocks, and tried to stir up a conversation with the young bartender.

"Hey! Would you know if Sophia and Nadia will be in the bar today?" He asked the young server.

"Who? The server feigned ignorance.

"Sophia and Nadia. They usually are present in this bar in the evenings," Hans spoke through clenched teeth.

"I wouldn't know, mate. Anyways, none of the girls here use their real name, you know. And their stage names change every day! Maybe talk to the other girls over there?" The bartender pointed him to a few other sensuous females sitting around the bar and chatting with the customers around them.

"No, not really. Thanks anyway," Hans concluded the conversation and decided to wait for his favourite girls. As his girls remained missing, his frustration steadily mounted. He desperately puffed on his cigarettes, downing drink after drink with an eagerness he had never felt before.

After a fairly long wait, which felt like eternity, during which Hans downed a few more whiskeys on the rocks, he was able to spot a familiar silhouette of a woman. It was Sophia!

Hans waved frantically towards her, and she gave him a seductive, sleepy smile as she came over.

"Hey, handsome!" Sophia greeted him with a sensuous smile, her hand trailing down his arm.

Hans nodded, his voice low and husky. "Where is Nadia please? We need to talk urgently."

Sofia leaned in closer, her breath warm against his ear, smelling of cheap alcohol. "Is it only talk, or you need more hard action, my lover boy!" She giggled uncontrollably.

It was clear to Hans that Sophia was already high on coke and alcohol and she was in no state for any serious discussion. Probably, she didn't even know if Nadia was with some other customer, or not in the bar today at all.

Everything was going wrong for Hans now. He ordered a drink for Sophia and gestured to her to sit next to him while they waited for Nadia.

Sophia continued to drink heavily like a thirsty traveller, while she kept murmuring sweet nothings in Hans ears. Right now, Hans was in no mood for this chit-chat. He started sweating profusely as night went by and there was no sign of Nadia.

Suddenly, he saw something which made his heart leap. Familiar busty blonde figure, waving over club patrons, and blowing kisses in the air. It was Nadia!

She came over, and glanced a very sexual look at him.

"How's my baby today?" She giggled as she waved at Hans and nodded at Sophia.

"I need to discuss something urgent. And I need you and Sophia with me tonight," begged Hans.

"Not tonight, my lover boy! I have a reservation with a very wealthy Zurich businessman. He buys diamonds and stuff for me and wants to marry me," giggled Nadia, obviously under heavy influence of coke and alcohol.

Hans' heart sank further, as the two girls were making him go crazy with their antics. He still needed his sexual release. He was addicted to the dark and uninhibited games he plays with these girls in the seedy hotel rooms. He desperately needed his mock revenge on Anna. He felt out of control with his current situation.

He decided to play it rough with them. He held the two girls with their elbows and pushed them out of the bar with force.

"Hey, hey! Take it easy with the girl man," he heard the bartender shout after him, but Hans was in no mood to indulge him.

Girls giggled as they moved out of the bar and to the nearby hotel where they had met before. The neon lights flickered overhead as they made their way through the dimly lit streets. He struggled to get the two drunk girls into the small seedy room, which plays the epicentre of his dark fantasies.

Hans's mind was a whirlwind of anger, frustration and unmet carnal desire by now. His evening was already a washout with the girls playing tantrums and he was already losing patience with everything going wrong in his life.

He decided to take it out on the girls tonight. They have to pay for their bad behaviour.

In the privacy of the hotel room, Hans felt the weight of his obsession pressing down on him. He took out his remaining wad of cash and threw it towards Nadia's and Sophia.

Girls giggled uncontrollably as they collected the bills spilled all over the bed and on the floor. The money was unusually larger than last time, and the girls realised they needed to make the night really special for Hans.

Nadia opened her purse, took out a small plastic bag, half filled with the usual white powder and drew multiple lines of coke on the bedroom table. Two girls, then proceeded to lick and inhale the powder with much abandon, to enjoy their night and let go of any inhibitions. Hans followed after them, as his mind swirled in the forbidden chemical pleasures.

Sofia and Nadia, now fully charged up, and aware of Hans' dark desires, began to transform themselves into the object of his fantasies. They changed into the classy clothes that resembled Anna's, adopting her mannerisms and voice.

Nadia came forward first, dressed as sophisticated Anna and started crawling towards Hans on her knees. She was aware of Hans' frustration and tried to make it up to him. She started licking Hans' boots and made seductive purr sounds while she licked hungrily and shook her booty seductively.

Hans felt a surge of power and excitement. The two slave girls in Anna's demeanour, crawling before him and begging for forgiveness is what he really needed. His manhood began to grow and he enjoyed the sight of Nadia crawling, bending and begging in front of him.

"I need Sophia first tonight," Hans hissed, as he caught hold of Nadia by her hair and pushed her away.

Sophia, her demure expression and petite frame, shook with fear as she realised it was her turn to take the treatment from Hans. She crawled forward, approached Hans on her fours.

She slowly raised herself to face Hans' manhood, now in its full glory, and begged seductively, "I am sorry for what I did master. Can I please lick you tonight and make you come on my face? Will that be fine as punishment, tonight?"

The line between reality and fantasy blurred, and Hans found himself lost in the dark scenario he had created.

Hans held Sophia's soft hair and slapped her face a few times with all his force, while his manhood was buried deep in her throat. Her already swollen cheeks slowly turned a few shades of crimson.

"Please, Hans," she begged, her voice trembling. "Hurt me more."

The words sent a shiver down Hans' spine, and he felt a rush of arousal. He grabbed her head roughly, his hands shaking with excitement. He threw her on the bed, and started taking off his dark leather belt. Perhaps, it was time for some serious punishment.

Nadia, playing the role of an observer, watched with wide eyes, her presence heightening the intensity of the encounter. Under the influence of coke and alcohol, they were more subservient, more than willing to indulge Hans's every whim.

Hans's mind was a whirlpool of rage and frustration as he waved his belt. The previous week's mounting failures fueled his dark thoughts. Desperation gnawed at him, morphing him into a very sinister person. The yesteryear's sophisticated writer was now a tormentor of whores in the cheap dark hotel rooms. His eyes gleamed with uncontrollable passion and lust as he sought to punish the naked girls lying eagle spread in front of him.

They had caused him enough trouble tonight, and he was determined to assert control, and so punishment became a dark, perverse necessity.

Hans wound his belt around his hand, preparing to lash the petite Sophia. She watched the madness in his eyes, fearfully staring at the leather waving in front of her face as she lay eagle-spread, vulnerable and naked on the bed. The lashings would be a serious punishment for her small frame.

Hans's grip tightened on the belt, his eyes dark with unrestrained fury. He felt a twisted sense of justice coursing through him. These girls had almost derailed his plans, and mocked his desperation with their frivolity.

His mind, clouded by anger and unmet carnal desires, convinced him that this punishment was necessary. He needed to assert dominance, to feel some semblance of control amidst the chaos of his crumbling life.

Only by releasing his pent-up rage could he regain the clarity and composure needed for his final plans. The belt cracked through the air, a grim testament to his spiralling descent into darkness and landed on Sophia's naked thighs.

Sophia's initial fear gave way to a surprising sense of exhilaration. Despite the stinging pain of the belt, or perhaps because of it, she began to revel in the rough treatment. Her flesh turned crimson, each belt strike leaving a vivid mark, but the intensity of the experience brought a twisted pleasure to her coke-fuelled mind.

Hans's forceful demeanour contrasted sharply with her other clients, and she found herself drawn to his dark, unrestrained, pent up energy.

As Hans continued, Sophia's screams morphed from pain to pleasure, echoing through the room with a fervent intensity. She arched her back, pushing into each strike, craving more of the raw, visceral punishment that Hans had unleashed.

Hans, driven by his own desperate need for control and release, was relentless. Each crack of the belt was a cathartic outlet for his pent-up rage. The room pulsed with a dark, primal energy, and all three of them were lost in the perverse dance of dominance and submission.

Hans's actions became more brutal, each movement fueled by his dark fantasies. He imagined that it was Anna beneath him, and it was her body that was writhing in pain. He enjoyed the power he felt, the control he had over Anna. Each swing of the belt, each harsh word coming out of his mouth, was a manifestation of his need to dominate and destroy Anna.

The more brutal he became, the more excited he felt, and his arousal reached newer heights. Hans kept lashing Sophia, while she begged for more, and Nadia rallied with cries of "Harder.. Harder!"

As Nadia watched the brutal encounter, she couldn't help but become part of the twisted scene. Her eyes gleamed with dark excitement as she played with both Sophia and Hans, her hands roaming over their naked bodies and her mouth hungrily covering Hans' manhood.

She cheered them on, her voice a seductive whisper, urging them to go further, while she pleasured herself, caught in the throes of their perverse game.

After satisfying himself with the belt lashings, Hans craved something more personal. His mind conjured images of his hands around Anna's throat, now played by Sophia. He wanted to deliver more serious punishment to her fragile body.

Hans's fingers wrapped around Sophia's neck, the contact electrifying. His grip tightened, and his eyes dark with intensity. Sophia, initially shocked, found herself drawn to the sensation, and the lack of absolute control was thrilling her.

Sophia's breaths became shallow as Hans's grip tightened, her wide eyes a mix of fear and excitement. The choking pressure on her throat sent a perverse rush through her body, heightening her drug fuelled senses.

Her pulse quickened, and she revelled in the twisted intimacy of the moment. Hans, lost in his dark fantasy, felt a surge of power, each choke a release of his pent-up rage and frustration. Sophia's muffled moans filled the room, blending with the heavy atmosphere of their shared, perverse game.

She begged for even harder treatment, encouraging the perverse game already being played. Her eyes widened with horror as she struggled for breath, but Hans, consumed by his dark desires, only squeezed her throat harder, revelling in her helplessness and fear.

Each cry and gasp from Sophia became a twisted echo of Anna's imagined suffering for him, and Hans enjoyed the power and control he felt. His brain was a storm of sadistic delight, relishing every moment of this cruel fantasy fulfilled.

The seedy hotel room was a shadowy den of debauchery, the air thick with the scent of sweat and lust. Their clothes lay on the floor, torn and discarded in a haphazard heap, remnants of their frenzied passion. Fabric was ripped and destroyed, buttons scattered, evidence of the violent madness that had overtaken them in this roleplay.

Suddenly, during the heights of the frenzied roleplay, Sophia let out a sharp cry and her body went limp. Her eyes were drawn out of her sockets, as she slumped onto the bed, with her head thrown back and body still. For a moment, there was a shocked silence in the room.

"Sophia?" Nadia's voice was filled with panic. She rushed to her friend's side, shaking her gently. "Sophia, wake up!"

Hans was frozen, his breath caught up in his throat as he realised that his bad luck was never going to leave him, even for a moment. He watched helplessly as Nadia quickly rummaged through her bag, pulling out a small vial and a syringe. Her hands trembled as she filled the syringe and injected Sophia's arm with the powerful medicine.

"Come on, Sophia, wake up," Nadia whispered urgently, her eyes wide with fear.

Hans was trembling with fear and sweating heavily, as he did not want Sophia to die in this shady room, under these circumstances. He wanted Anna to suffer and die, and not the random prostitute he found in Zurich's lanes. Tonight was definitely not his night.

After a few tense moments, Sophia's body shook and her eyes fluttered open. She took a deep, shuddering breath, her body trembling. "I'm okay," she mumbled, her voice weak. "I'm okay."

Nadia let out a sigh of relief, her hands still shaking. She turned to Hans, her pale face a mix of anger and concern. "You need to be more careful, Hans. We can't keep doing this if it means killing her like this."

Hans nodded, his mind racing. The sight of Sophia's unconscious body had jolted him back to reality, if only for a moment. "I'm sorry. I didn't mean to go that far."

Sophia, still lying on the bed, gave a perverse smile. "It's okay. Just... don't stop." She begged again to keep the game on. "Please, Hans, finish the game!"

Hans, engulfed by his dark urges, let out a primal groan, which escalated to a frenzied scream as he penetrated Sophia's naked body with ferocious intensity. Each thrust grew more brutal, driven by his manic desperation. The room echoed with the girl's lustful cries, creating a chilling symphony of unrestrained madness.

Hans's hands struck the soft bodies of Nadia and Sophia beneath him, each slap resonating in the dimly lit room. Their flesh quivered under the force of his blows, mingling with the sounds of their laboured breaths and his fervent grunts. His movements were relentless, fueled by a dark, insatiable hunger.

In a final surge of perverse ecstasy, Hans reached his climax, releasing with a shuddering groan. His body convulsed as he splashed the two girls' faces with his come, their glistening bodies now marked by his dark satisfaction. The room fell silent except for their ragged breaths, the aftermath of their twisted encounter hanging heavy in the air.

The girls lay beside Hans, breathing heavily, their eyes half-closed with exhaustion. "So, what's the plan now?" Nadia asked, her voice hoarse.

Hans took a deep breath, trying to clear his mind. "I spent all my money on the Albanian goons and they failed miserably. We need to find a new approach. The police are watching, and Anna is on high alert. We need to be smarter."

Sofia nodded, her expression thoughtful. "Maybe we can use someone else. Someone she wouldn't suspect. We need to get close to her, and find her weaknesses."

Hans considered her words, a dark smile playing on his lips. "Yes. We need to find a way to get inside her life, make her trust someone who can get the job done for us."

As they lay together in the dimly lit room, their naked bodies entwined, Hans felt a renewed sense of purpose.

The darkness within him was strong, and he was determined to find a way to destroy Anna, no matter what it takes.

CHAPTER 27

Pushed to the Edge

The lustful encounter with Sofia and Nadia had left Hans feeling more desperate and unhinged than ever. The failures of his hired goons gnawed at him, and the brutal roleplay had only temporarily satiated his dark desires.

As the three lay together on the dimly lit hotel room bed, Sofia and Nadia exchanged a glance, a silent agreement passing between them. It was time to push Hans further, to convince him to take matters into his own hands.

Hans lay between Sofia and Nadia, the adrenaline of the roleplay still pulsing through his veins. He stared at the ceiling, his mind still racing with the images of Anna's imagined suffering. Sofia propped herself up on one elbow, her fingers lightly tracing circles on Hans's chest.

"Hans," she began softly, her voice filled with a dangerous allure, "You have tried everything, but nothing seems to work."

Hans sighed, frustration evident in his voice. "I know. It is like she is this invincible bitch, who always wins."

Nadia, lying on his other side, leaned in closer. "Maybe it's time to stop relying on others, Hans. Maybe it's time to take control for yourself."

Hans turned to look at her, confusion and curiosity in his eyes. "What do you mean?"

Sofia's fingers continued their lazy circles, her touch both soothing and suggestive. "Think about it, Hans. You have the power, you have the drive. We felt it tonight. You need to take matters into your own hands. Punish Anna yourself."

Hans shook his head, a mixture of fear and excitement coursing through him. "I don't know. It's different to actually do it myself. It is... dangerous."

Nadia's eyes gleamed in the dim light. "But that's what excites you, isn't it? The danger, the control. We felt it tonight. Imagine how much more powerful it would be to do it for real."

Hans's mind raced with the possibilities, the thrill of the idea taking root. He imagined Anna's face, her fear, her helplessness. The thought sent a shiver down his spine, both terrifying and exhilarating.

Sofia leaned closer, her lips brushing against his ear. "You want to see Anna suffer, Hans. You want to be the one to end her. You know you do."

Hans closed his eyes, his breath coming in short, ragged gasps. "I... I don't know."

Nadia's hand slid down his chest, her touch igniting a fire within him. "You do know. You just need to embrace it. Think about the pleasure, the satisfaction. No more failures. No more relying on others."

Hans's resistance began to crumble under their combined influence. The dark fantasies that had consumed him for so long now seemed within reach, tangible and real.

Sofia and Nadia continued their seductive assault, their words and touches a dangerous mix of encouragement and temptation.

"You've always wanted this, Hans," Sofia whispered. "You just need to take the final step. Be the master of your fate. Take what is yours."

Hans opened his eyes, the desire and fear warring within him. "But... what if I get caught?"

Nadia's smile was predatory. "You won't get caught. We will help you. We can plan it perfectly, make sure there are no loose ends."

Sofia nodded in agreement. "We'll be with you every step of the way. You won't be alone."

Hans felt his resolve weakening, the allure of their words drawing him in. He imagined the scene, the power and control he would feel. The ultimate act of domination. It was intoxicating.

"Alright," he said finally, his voice trembling with anticipation and fear. "I'll do it. But we need a plan. A perfect plan."

Sofia and Nadia exchanged a triumphant glance, their eyes gleaming with excitement. "We'll help you, Hans," Sofia said, her voice soothing. "We'll make sure everything goes smoothly."

They spent the next few hours discussing the plan, each detail meticulously crafted. Hans listened intently, his mind filled with a dark excitement. The more they talked, the more real it became, and the more he craved the power and control it would bring.

As the first light of dawn began to filter through the curtains, Hans felt a strange sense of calm. The decision had been made, the plan set in motion. He would take matters into his own hands, reclaim the power and control he had lost.

Sofia and Nadia lay beside him, their presence a constant source of encouragement and support. "You are ready, Hans," Sofia whispered. "You can do this."

Hans nodded, his mind filled with dark determination. "I will. I'll make sure she never escapes."

As they drifted off to a much-needed sleep, Hans's dreams were filled with images of Anna's final moments, the thrill of the kill, and the power he would finally reclaim. The darkness within him was strong, and he was ready to embrace it fully.

The path ahead was dangerous, but he was determined to see it through. There was no turning back now. The ultimate act of control and domination awaited him, and he was ready to take it.

As the details of their dark plan solidified in his mind, Hans found himself overwhelmed with a mix of fear, excitement, and arousal. The thought of finally having the power to end Anna's life consumed him, filling him with a perverse thrill.

Alone in the dimly lit room, Hans's breath quickened as he envisioned the scene; Anna's terrified eyes, her desperate struggles, and his triumphant control over her. Unable to resist the dark pull of his fantasies, he reached down and touched his manhood, his hand moving with increasing urgency.

The vivid images in his mind—her fear, his dominance—pushed him over the edge, and he shuddered with a twisted sense of satisfaction, his body convulsing as he gave in to the dark pleasure of his imaginings.

As Hans started rubbing himself, Sofia and Nadia watched him with a mix of fascination and amusement. Their eyes gleamed in the dim light as they observed his every movement, and found the intensity of his arousal captivating.

When he finally shuddered with orgasmic release, they exchanged knowing glances. Sofia leaned in close, her voice a seductive whisper, "Looks like you enjoyed the plan a bit too much, Hans."

Nadia chuckled softly, her hand trailing lightly down his chest. "Just wait until you get to do it for real. This was just a trailer."

Their teasing words and sly smiles only served to deepen his obsession, consuming Hans completely.

CHAPTER 28

The Night of the Revenge

The evening was dark, sinister, and quiet as Hans, Sofia, and Nadia waited in a parked car near Anna's home. They waited patiently for a few hours, each taking turns to drink from Hans' whisky flask and talking to each other in silent whispers as they bided their time.

Finally, Hans alerted the two girls as they saw a car moving in the parking lot. They quietly watched as Anna and Lukas stepped out, ending their pleasurable night out, their laughter filling the night air.

Hans felt a surge of anger and anticipation. He watched tensely as Lukas kissed Anna goodnight passionately, reversed his car, and left, unaware of the danger lurking nearby.

As Lukas left, Anna moved inside her home. Hans, Nadia, and Sophia, carefully watching her, now moved swiftly. Hans and the two girls approached the back door of Anna's new home under the cover of darkness.

They worked quickly, using a set of tools Nadia had procured from her shady bar customers. Nadia, with her nimble fingers, picked the lock while Hans and Sophia kept watch. The faint click of the lock yielding sent a thrill through them, a shared moment of silent triumph.

With the door now unlocked, they moved stealthily inside. The girls' movements were practised and efficient, a testament to their illicit criminal skills.

Hans's heart pounded with a mix of nervous fear and exhilaration as they entered the house. The dimly lit interior seemed to welcome them into its shadows, each step bringing them closer to the culmination of their dangerous plan.

They navigated through the unfamiliar layout, their breaths held tight, ready for the next phase of their dark mission.

Anna, slightly drunk and tired, was on the living room couch with her eyes closed, unaware of their ghastly presence and devious plans.

Sofia and Nadia approached Anna with devilish smiles. "Anna, you look so exhausted, dear. How about you take a nice, relaxing bath while we keep you company?" Sofia whispered smoothly.

Anna, despite her drowsy state from the alcohol, got a jolt and was wide awake immediately. She sensed the immense danger, and her eyes widened with fear as she realised the unwelcome presence of Hans and the two strange women in her home.

Nadia took out a handkerchief heavily laced with a powerful sedative as she covered Anna's face while Sophia and Hans pinned her one arm each to prevent her from struggling.

It was a tremendous effort for the three of them to control Anna, as she kicked, moved around, and gave them everything to break free. After a while, the sedative's effect started showing, and Anna's struggle started becoming weaker.

Hans and Sofia grabbed Anna by her shoulders and forced her towards the bathroom, while Nadia pushed her from behind.

Anna's attempts to fight back were futile against their combined strength, and the sedative was gradually breaking down her resistance.

With a final, desperate cheer, the trio pushed Anna into the bathtub, the water splashing violently as she fell in, setting the stage for their cruel intentions.

Hans, unable to resist his dark desires, now began to dominate the situation. He knelt by the tub, his eyes dark with intent. "Anna," he uttered softly, "Let's talk about us. Let's make things right."

Anna, drowsy from the combined effect of alcohol and sedatives, was barely able to open her eyes. "Hans, what are you doing here?" she murmured, her words slightly slurred.

Sofia and Nadia exchanged uneasy glances but went along with Hans's plan. They thrust a flask of whiskey to Anna's mouth, pushing her to drink more.

"Relax, Anna. We're just here to help," Nadia said soothingly.

Hans's mind raced with his dark desires. He wanted to savour the moment, to draw out Anna's fear and helplessness, and to torture her. He began to stroke her hair, his touch gentle, but his eyes cold. "Just relax, Anna. Everything will be fine," he whispered.

As Anna gulped the whiskey forcefully, her eyes grew heavier. She leaned back in the tub, closing her eyes.

Nadia, growing impatient, leaned in and whispered urgently, "Hans, we need to finish her. Now!"

Hans could feel his control slipping, his desire to dominate overwhelming him. He wanted to take his time, to enjoy every moment of Anna's fear and submission.

Hans shook his head, his voice low and menacing, his hands traversing Anna's sensuous and wet body, "Not yet. I'm not done yet."

Hans's touches became more invasive, his hands entering Anna's wet dress and trailing down her body with a possessive hunger. He whispered cruel taunts in her ear, reminding her of past betrayals and his hatred towards her.

Anna, too sedated to fully comprehend what was happening, weakly tried to push him away, but her efforts were completely futile.

Hans's excitement grew as he watched Anna's futile struggles. He forced her head down, holding her underwater for a few seconds before pulling her up, letting her gasp desperately for some air.

The terror in Anna's eyes, her gasp for air, fueled his perverse pleasure. He repeated this act several times, savouring each moment of her desperation. Anna's breath was heavy and short as she struggled to stay alive.

Sofia and Nadia watched in horror, realising the depth of Hans's depravity. Nadia tried to intervene. "Hans, there is no time for this foreplay. We need to finish her now."

But Hans was beyond reasoning. He held Anna's head underwater again, this time longer than before. Her struggles weakened, and Hans felt a twisted sense of satisfaction in her pain.

As Anna lay half-submerged in the tub, her eyes barely opening with a mix of drowsiness and fear, Hans's dark desires surged within him. The sight of her vulnerable state, completely at his mercy, ignited a perverse thrill that he could no longer resist.

With a twisted smile, he began to undress his trousers, his hands trembling with a sick anticipation. He relished in the thought of satisfying his twisted cravings one last time, his gaze fixed on Anna's barely conscious form, wet and naked in the water.

The sound of his clothes hitting the floor echoed in the dimly lit bathroom, a sinister prelude to the depravity he was about to unleash.

Sofia and Nadia, realising the time they were losing, tried to intervene, their voices filled with panic.

"Hans, this is no time to have sex with her! We need to finish her now!" Sofia pleaded, stepping towards him.

But Hans, consumed by his twisted desire, turned on them with a ferocious snarl. He slapped Sofia hard across the face, sending her staggering back, and then struck Nadia's face with equal force, silencing their protests.

The raw power in his slaps cowed them into submission, their fear palpable as they watched Hans, now fully naked, move towards the defenceless Anna with a desperate, predatory hunger.

Hans, in a frenzy of desperation and dark desire, entered the tub, grasped Anna's wet and limp body, and started forcing himself upon her. As he started ravaging her, the reality of his actions began to seep in.

The thrill he once desperately sought was now overshadowed by an overwhelming sense of defeat and loss. He realised, in that twisted moment of brutality, that his life was spiralling beyond redemption.

His career, his sanity, his very essence—everything was collapsing around him. Sofia and Nadia watched in horror, their faces pale and eyes wide with shock, as Hans's actions painted a stark picture of a man who had crossed every line and still lost, knowing deep down that his end was near.

Hans, now completely unhinged and beyond any hope of redemption, turned to Sofia and Nadia with wild, hungry eyes.

"Join us," he demanded, his voice a chilling mix of desperation and madness. The two girls, paralyzed with fear and revulsion, hesitated at the edge of the tub, their horror mounting as they watched Hans continue his perverse acts.

Hans started crying and howling loudly as he thrusted deep inside Anna, the sounds echoing off the bathroom walls, creating a nightmarish symphony of despair. Each sob and scream was a testament to his broken mind, a man who had lost all semblance of sanity.

Sofia and Nadia, trembling, realised they were now trapped in a macabre scene from which there was no easy escape, their fear deepening with every passing second.

Hans, driven by a twisted mix of desperation and hatred, came heavily inside the barely conscious Anna, her naked body lying limp in the now-cold water.

His cries of anguish and anger echoed through the bathroom as he satisfied his perverse desires, tears streaming down his face. Sofia and Nadia, standing frozen with horror, could only watch the horrifying scene unfold.

Once his dark urges were sated, Hans's perverse thoughts boiled over again. He stood up, his face contorted with a sick combination of triumph and despair.

With a vicious snarl, he grabbed Anna by the hair, forcing her head finally underwater.

"You worthless, ungrateful bitch!" he screamed, his voice raw with fury. "This is what you deserve!"

Anna's body jerked weakly in the water as Hans held her down, shouting a torrent of abuses and profanities.

The cold water splashed around them, mingling with his tears and the sweat of his exertion.

Sofia and Nadia, too terrified to intervene, watched in stunned silence as life slowly drained from Anna's body, Hans's words growing more incoherent and frenzied.

The bathroom became a chamber of nightmares, filled with the sounds of his deranged howling and the sickening sight of his final, monstrous act.

Just as Anna's struggles began to weaken significantly, a knock on the home front door startled them. Hans looked up, his heart pounding. The front door creaked open, and Lukas's cheerful voice called out, "Anna? I forgot to give you something."

Panic surged through Hans, Sofia, and Nadia, and they exchanged frantic looks.

"We have to go!" Nadia hissed.

Hans quickly lifted Anna's head out of the water. She was unconscious, but still breathing faintly. He was now trying to bring up his pants in panic, as Lukas roamed the house looking for Anna.

Lukas's footsteps approached the living room and then towards the bathroom, the approaching sound growing louder.

Hans motioned for Sofia and Nadia to hide. He quickly staged the scene, placing the wine glass on the edge of the tub and making it look like Anna had slipped.

Lukas knocked on the bathroom door a few times and then slowly entered. His eyes widened in shock at the sight before him. "Anna!" he shouted, rushing to her side.

Hans, trying to appear calm, stepped back. "She must have slipped. I was just trying to help her relax."

Lukas got a jolt and he realised the evil presence of Han and two strange women in Anna's bathroom. He quickly realised what this setup was.

"What the hell are you doing here, Hans?" Lukas saw the fear in Anna's eyes and the remnants of her struggle. "You did this, didn't you?"

Hans backed away, realising Lukas was much younger and of a stronger build than him. Hans repeated Lukas' old dialogue to spite him, "Lukas, this is not what it looks like."

Lukas lunged at Hans, grabbing him by the collar. "You bastard! You tried to kill her!"

Hans fought back, the two men grappling and throwing punches at each other.

The bathroom was a whirlwind of chaos as Lukas and Hans grappled violently. Hans, fueled by rage and jealousy, swung wildly at Lukas, who fought back with equal ferocity.

The confined space amplified their struggle, with each man desperate to overpower the other. Tiles cracked, and toiletries scattered as their bodies slammed into walls and fixtures.

Hans's face contorted with fury, while Lukas's expression was one of steely determination. The sound of their heavy breathing and grunts echoed, creating a cacophony that mirrored the intensity of their brutal confrontation.

Sofia and Nadia, realising the plan was falling apart, tried to intervene, but Lukas's fury was unstoppable. Lukas landed a solid punch on Hans' jaw, sending him staggering backward.

Hans stumbled back, his mouth broken and bloody from the force of Lukas's punch, the metallic taste of blood mingling with his seething rage.

Realising he was outmatched and getting beaten up, Hans turned and bolted for the door.

"We need to get out of here!" Hans shouted to Sofia and Nadia as he fled the scene.

Hans ran through the dark streets, his breath coming in ragged gasps. He didn't stop until he was far from Anna's home, his mind reeling from the night's events.

The plan had failed spectacularly, and now he was on the run.

Sofia and Nadia followed closely behind, their faces pale with fear and frustration.

"What now, Hans?" Sofia, out of breath, while she ran fast, "We're screwed!"

Hans wiped the blood from his mouth, his mind racing. "We need to lay low. Find a place to hide until we can figure out our next move."

As they disappeared into the night, the weight of their actions settled heavily on them. Anna had escaped again. The darkness within Hans was stronger than ever, but now it was tempered with a new sense of desperation.

The path ahead was uncertain, and the consequences of their failed plan loomed large. But Hans knew one thing for certain: he couldn't give up. He had come too far, and the darkness within him demanded retribution.

Back at Anna's home, Lukas cradled her unconscious naked body, his mind racing with worry and anger. He called for an ambulance, praying that she would survive.

As the paramedics arrived and took Anna away, Lukas vowed to protect her at all costs. He knew Hans would stop at nothing, and he had to be ready for whatever came next.

As Hans, Sofia, and Nadia hid in the darkness of nearby Sihlwald forest, the game of cat and mouse continued.

The stakes were higher than ever, and the darkness within Hans was far from settled.

CHAPTER 29

The Final Descent

Sihlwald forest was shrouded in darkness as Hans, Sofia, and Nadia ran through the bushes, their breaths ragged and frantic. They could hear the police sirens from a distance, approaching Anna's home.

The moon cast an eerie glow on the twisted branches above, creating a sinister backdrop for their escape. The chilling silence of the night was interrupted only by their hurried footsteps and the occasional snap of twigs underfoot.

Finally, they stopped in a small clearing, with their hearts pounding in their chests. Nadia, her voice trembling but determined, broke the silence. "Hans, we have done our part. We deserve our share of the money."

Sophia, still pale from the horrifying events, nodded in agreement. "You promised us a lot of cash for this, Hans. We risked everything."

Hans, his eyes wild with residual fury, sneered at them. "You think you deserve anything? You are nothing but useless whores. I did all the work tonight. Besides, I am completely broke. I do not have any money."

Nadia's eyes flashed with anger. "We helped you, Hans. We were a part of this plan. You owe us the money!"

Hans's expression twisted into one of contempt. "I owe you nothing. You were lucky to even be a part of this. Now get out of my sight."

Nadia stepped forward, her fear turning into rage. "We won't leave without our money, Hans. We earned it."

Hans pushed Nadia away forcefully while angrily staring down at her. She was not the one to take it back lightly. She lunged at Hans with all her fury.

The forest erupted into chaos as the three of them lunged at each other, their desperation and anger boiling over.

Hans grabbed Nadia by the throat, shoving her against a tree with a force that left her gasping for air. Sophia tried to intervene, clawing at Hans's face, but he was too far gone in his rage to feel the pain.

With a brutal shove, Hans sent Sofia crashing to the ground. He turned his attention to Nadia, grabbing her by the hair and throwing her against a rock. She hit the ground hard, her body crumpling from the impact. Hans, his mind a whirlwind of dark thoughts, advanced on her with a twisted smile.

"You want your money?" he snarled, lifting Nadia to her feet only to slam her back down again. "Here is your cash payment."

Sofia, recovering from the initial assault, grabbed a large branch and swung it at Hans, hitting him in the face. Hans roared in pain and fury, then turned on her with a deadly intent. He wrestled the branch from her grasp and struck her with it, the sickening loud thud echoing in the forest.

Hans's strength and rage overwhelmed them both. He grabbed Sofia by the neck, punching her face and squeezing her throat until her struggles ceased. Sophia's eyes glazed over in lifelessness. He dropped her petite body to the ground with a thud, turning his attention back to Nadia, who was attempting to crawl away.

With a perverse satisfaction, Hans dragged Nadia's legs back, and his hands tightened around her throat. "You think you can get away from me, you bloody whore?" he hissed. "You're just as pathetic as Anna was."

Nadia's struggles grew weaker as Hans's grip tightened on her throat, his eyes filled with a crazed light. She scratched at his arms, leaving deep, bloody gouges, but it wasn't enough to stop him. Her life ebbed away, her final breaths choked out by Hans's relentless grasp.

Hans picked up a stone lying nearby and hammered both their heads with the fury of a madman. The stone turned red and sticky, but Hans kept hitting both the bodies till he was reasonably sure that neither of the two girls was alive.

Hans staggered back, his chest heaving, his body covered in scratches, blood, and bruises from the violent confrontation. He looked down at the two lifeless bodies, his mind numb with a mix of triumph and dark desire. The forest was silent now, the chaos giving way to an eerie stillness.

Hans was badly hurt and had barely survived. He limped to a nearby stream, staring at his reflection in the dark water.

His face was a mask of blood and rage, a twisted mockery of the man he once was.

He knew there was no going back from this. The dark desires within him had completely consumed him.

As he stood there, the full weight of his actions settled over him. He had killed Sofia and Nadia, each murder more brutal than the last. He didn't know whether Anna was alive or dead.

His life was a ruin, and he was alone in his madness. The realisation brought a bitter smile to his lips. In his quest for power and control, he had lost everything.

Hans turned away from the scene, his mind already working on his next move. He had to hide the girl's bodies and cover his tracks. The game of cat and mouse would continue, but now he was the only player left.

CHAPTER 30

The End

Hans ran through the Sihlwald forest crazily, with his breath coming in ragged gasps. The darkness of the night was pierced by the distant wail of approaching police sirens and the occasional flash of searchlights.

Panic gripped him as he stumbled over roots and underbrush, the sound of his pursuers growing closer. His body ached from the bruises and beating left by Lukas, Sofia, and Nadia, and the knowledge that he had left two dead bodies behind weighed heavily on his mind.

The vast Sihlwald forest seemed to close in around him, the shadows deepening as he pushed through the thick undergrowth. Every snap of a twig, every rustle of leaves sent a jolt of fear through him.

He felt as if he was running around in the vast forest on a circular path. His mind was going crazy with fear and panic, as his breaths were running short.

The police were relentless, their shouts echoing through the trees as they searched for Hans. Hans knew that if they caught him, there would be no escape from justice.

In a desperate bid to lose his pursuers, he veered off the path and plunged deeper into the forest. The terrain became rougher, the ground uneven and treacherous. He could hear the howls of wolves in the distance, a chilling reminder of the dangers that lurked in the darkness.

Slowly, the sirens and sounds started fading as he veered deeper into the Sihlwald forest. Hans realised he was finally able to dodge the police. He smiled at his luck.

No one can beat Hans, not just yet.

Hans slowed to a walk, his lungs burning and his legs trembling with exhaustion. He stumbled upon a small clearing and collapsed against a tree, trying to catch his breath. The police sirens were still barely audible, but they seemed very far away now.

He relaxed for a while under the tree as he gathered his thoughts. What if Anna survived? Will Lukas and Anna get married and live happily ever after, while he keeps running away from the police? What will the future entail? Hans kept thinking of endless questions circling in his head, as the forest turned darker and hummed with the night's rhythm.

He suddenly heard something strange and primal. The sounds of night forest hums mixed with the sharp howls of the wolves getting closer.

Hans's heart pounded in his chest as he realised he was not alone. From the shadows, a pack of wolves emerged, their eyes glowing in the dark with a predatory hunger. They circled him slowly, as he lay on the ground, tired, their growls hungry and menacing.

Hans scrambled to his feet, looking around desperately for a weapon. He grabbed a fallen branch, holding it out in front of him as the wolves closed in.

"Stay back, you bastards!" he shouted, his voice trembling with fear.

The wolves ignored his warning, their growls growing louder. Hans swung the branch wildly, managing to strike one of the wolves on the snout.

It yelped in pain but did not retreat. Instead, the pack lunged at him, with their sharp naked teeth and hungry claws.

Hans fought with a frenzied desperation of a madman, swinging the branch and kicking at the wolves. He managed to land a few blows, but the wolves were powerful and relentless.

They bit and clawed at him, their sharp teeth repeatedly tearing into his flesh. Hans screamed in pain as one wolf sank its teeth into his leg, dragging him to the ground as the other wolves closed in.

He continued to fight, using the branch and his fists to fend off the attackers. But the wolves were too many, and his strength was failing.

Blood started pouring freely from his wounds, staining the forest floor. Each bite and claw mark sapped his energy, and his vision began to blur.

Hans lay on the forest ground, the wolves now retreating into the shadows, their hunger sated with his flesh. He was alone now, his body broken from countless deep wounds and bites, and he was bleeding profusely. He could barely breathe as the pain started taking over his consciousness.

He looked up at the sky, the distant horizon tinged with the fading light of the setting sun. The realisation of his imminent death washed over him, bringing a strange sense of calm.

As the darkness closed in, Hans thought of Anna, Sofia, and Nadia. He had sought power and control over the women in his life, but in the end, it had led to his destruction.

The forest around him grew silent, the police sirens and searchlights a distant memory. He was alone with his thoughts, his regrets, and the cold embrace of death.

The sun was below the horizon, casting the forest into deep shadows of the night. Hans' breathing grew shallow, his life slipping away with each ragged breath.

He closed his eyes, surrendering to the darkness. The final reckoning had come, and there was no escaping it. The Sihlwald forest, once a place of terror and violence, became his final resting place as the night enveloped him in its cold embrace.

Hans' mind, desperate to escape the current agony, drifted into a dreamlike state. The darkness of the forest melted away, replaced by a vision of a happier time in the past.

In his hallucination, Hans dreamt of Anna and himself on a beautiful Swiss countryside vacation. They were walking hand in hand through lush green meadows, the snow-capped Alps standing majestically in the background.

The air was fresh and filled with the scent of wildflowers. Anna's carefree laughter echoed around them, filling Hans with a profound sense of joy.

They stopped by a crystal-clear lake, its surface shimmering under the warm sunlight. Anna turned to him, her eyes sparkling with love. "Isn't this perfect, Hans?" she asked, her voice gentle and full of affection.

Hans nodded, a genuine smile spreading across his face. "Yes, Anna. It's perfect," he replied, his heart swelling with happiness. In this dream, there was no anger, no bitterness—only love and contentment. They embraced, and for a moment, all the darkness that had consumed his life seemed to vanish.

As the hallucination continued, Hans and Anna found themselves in a cosy chalet nestled in the mountains. They sat by the fireplace, the warmth of the flames wrapping around them. Anna leaned her head on Hans's shoulder, and he felt a deep sense of peace and fulfilment.

"I love you, Anna," he whispered, his voice filled with genuine emotion. She looked up at him, her eyes brimming with love. "I love you too, Hans," she replied, her words a soothing balm to his tortured soul. They embraced each other passionately in an eternal hug.

Hans's breathing grew shallow, his life now slipping away. His vision of Anna became clearer, more vivid, as if she were truly there with him.

With his last bit of strength, Hans muttered, "Anna... Anna... I love you, Anna." His voice was barely a whisper, carried away by the gentle breeze that rustled the leaves above.

Hans took one last, shuddering breath, and then he was still forever. The name of the woman he had loved and ought to destroy lingered on his lips, a bittersweet end to his life consumed by his dark desires.

The forest around him grew silent, in the night's shadows, casting a final darkness over the world he had left behind.

The wolves moved in again, eager to satiate their hunger with the remnants of Hans' body.

Acknowledgements

I extend my heartfelt gratitude to my family for their unwavering support and belief in me throughout this book-writing journey—a special thanks to Shantanu Ray Chaudhuri, whose editorial expertise and insightful guidance have been invaluable. I also deeply appreciate Rhea Gangavkar for her meticulous attention to detail and thoughtful feedback, which enriched the narrative. I sincerely thank Mr Ajay Mago of Om Books for his guidance and support during this journey. Their combined efforts have been instrumental in bringing *Dark Desires* to life.